AN EXTRAO
OF COUR
AND HUMANITY

In the spring of 1839, fifty-three African captives, led by Cinque, revolt on board the Spanish slave ship *Amistad*. Captured off the Eastern Seaboard, they find themselves strangers in a strange land and victims of the American system and its president, Martin Van Buren. Struggling for his own reelection, Van Buren is willing to sacrifice the Africans to appease the pro-slavery South. The Africans are joined in their fight by lawyer Roger Baldwin, abolitionist Ted Joadson, and former president John Quincy Adams, who carry their battle all the way to the United States Supreme Court. It is a case that questions the very foundation of the American legal system—and celebrates the ultimate triumph of the human spirit.

AMISTAD

A NOVEL BY ALEXS PATE
BASED ON THE SCREENPLAY
BY DAVID FRANZONI

DREAMWORKS

SIGNET
Published by the Penguin Group
Penguin Putnam Inc., 375 Hudson Street,
New York, New York 10014, U.S.A.
Penguin Books Ltd, 27 Wrights Lane,
London W8 5TZ, England
Penguin Books Australia Ltd,
Ringwood, Victoria, Australia
Penguin Books Canada Ltd, 10 Alcorn Avenue,
Toronto, Ontario, Canada M4V 3B2
Penguin Books (N.Z.) Ltd, 182–190 Wairau Road,
Auckland 10, New Zealand

Penguin Books Ltd, Registered Offices:
Harmondsworth, Middlesex, England

First published by Signet, an imprint of Dutton Signet,
a member of Penguin Putnam Inc.

First Printing, December, 1997
10 9 8 7 6

Ⓓ REGISTERED TRADEMARK—MARCA REGISTRADA

Printed in the United States of America

Acknowledgments

I want to give my respect and thanks to Debbie Allen and Steven Spielberg for making this project happen. I was guided by two wise and capable editors, Anne McGrath at DreamWorks and Danielle Perez at Dutton Signet. And where would I be without Faith Childs, my agent, who is the light at the end of the tunnel or at least a true reflection of it? I would also like to thank Macalester College history professor Peter Rachleff for his generous time and materials which were of tremendous help. Thanks also to Me-K. Ahn, Gyanni Pate, Ralph Remington, John Wright, Serena Wright, David Mura, Susan Sensor, J. Otis Powell, Archie Givens, Carol Givens, Jean Anne Durades, Wanda Pate, Kimlar Satterthwaite, Napoleon Andrews, Joel Baer, Anthony Pinn, and Richard Ammons.

Finally, I dedicate this book to my mother, Lois Pate, who still stands as an example of ferocious life.

A Note about the Chapter Epigrams

The epigrams at the beginning of many of the chapters are Mende proverbs. They were taken from *Klo Klo Lo A N'ja Ve (Little Drops of Water Flood the River: The Peoples' Educational Association Stories and Songs from Sierra Leone)*. They were largely compiled by Arthur Abraham and Abibu Tamu.

Prologue

The darkened sky spoke sweetly as they slept. The stars, like cinders, glowed. But something caused Sengbe Pieh (who would come to be called Cinque) to wake up abruptly. Perhaps it was the powerful stillness that had settled around them. He could hear no sound outside his cone-shaped, thatched-roof house. This was quite unusual because he lived on the edge of his village, so close to the swampy forests and jungle which began just beyond. The predawn morning was usually alive with the sounds of foraging animals on the hunt, the ever-present chatter of the monkeys and the call of various birds.

Sengbe, a tall, twenty-four-year-old, muscular man who could hide among ebony and not be detected, pulled himself from his bed. He didn't even take the time to put on his protective charms, but moved gently so as not to disturb his wife and sleeping children. When he reached the threshold he could feel his thumping heart. He stepped out into the clearing. He felt a presence. There was something or someone nearby. And then Sengbe saw it. A lion. It stood only twenty-five or thirty feet away. He almost mistook the scene for a dream. Perhaps he was still asleep, curled up next to his wife.

Sengbe's immediate instinct was to shout for his wife to wake up and run away—to disappear, to do something that would take her and his three children completely out of harm's way. But he stopped himself. The animal just stood there watching Sengbe.

He recognized the lion as one that had, for some unexplained reason, taken up residence near their village. This was already quite unusual. But to make matters worse, this lion had a bad reputation, as lions will when they become man-eaters. The whole village was afraid; two people had already been killed. And several hunting expeditions had come back unsuccessful.

The lion stood motionless, itself like an image carved in wood. Sengbe suddenly felt the sweat pouring from his brow. What was it he was supposed to do? He had dreamed of being a brave warrior or a great hunter. Which, in a way, was amusing because though he thought of himself as brave, he was not by nature violent at all. And with the lion staring at him, he was almost petrified with fear. He had stupidly left his knife and walking staff behind. He would never be able to retrieve them in time. And even if he could, what good would they be? He felt panic rising in his chest.

But Sengbe was the type of man who could transform panic into something else. He looked back at his hut. He thought about his wife and children. They were in real danger if the animal overcame him. Would it continue on?

At his right foot was a smooth gray stone the size of his palm. He picked it up.

At this movement, the lion smiled at him and slowly approached. And then suddenly it began to gallop and Sengbe realized it wasn't his family who was in immediate danger. It was he. The lion was coming for him. And in a flash, Sengbe reached back—the rock heavy enough for him to worry whether he could control its flight—and hurled it at the approaching lion, hitting it right between the eyes. It fell instantly. Now, it was once again motionless.

Sengbe sat down hard on the ground. His wife, Tafe, came running with his two-year-old son. Sengbe looked up as he struggled to breathe. He realized that this was the first time he had breathed since he'd seen the lion. He looked at the big cat lying there motionless. It was then he finally put the picture together in his mind. Then it was funny. Not falling-down hysterical—but funny, and he smiled. "I think the lion is dead," he said.

She kneeled close to him, smiled, and threw her arms around him. "Yes, Sengbe, you have killed the lion."

And from this moment, whenever people talked of Sengbe, they were quick to add the label of "lion killer." The story was often told or danced at celebrations. Among the villagers it became folklore. But Sengbe often felt uncomfortable with such attention. Yes, he had killed the lion. But he had done it with a stone and not with a spear. And he had done it because he was scared to death that the lion would kill him. There was nothing heroic about that. So he accepted his new reputation with great humbleness, even deference. "Please do not make too much of this," he seemed to say. "I was just lucky."

But of course his people were grateful and made many gifts to him. He was given land, livestock, and other presents. But Sengbe couldn't help but feel a little guilty about the attention being given to him. In the evening as he sat with his family, the night breeze bringing invigorating, regenerating air through the trees just beyond, he would sadly but thankfully admit that were it not for the lion, he would not have so large a farm.

I
Rebellion

"It is time for us to rise, rise up."

Whenever trouble threatened, Sengbe, now called Cinque, always relied on two things to give him strength. A *gris-gris* charm his wife had given him that he'd managed to hold on to and the memory of how he'd killed the lion. One was protection and hope; the other a true moment of bravery. But the trouble he was in now seemed beyond the power of anything to save him. And yet he was not ready to give in.

His entire reality had been replaced by chains and the stifling air of slave ships. He'd been plucked from his life in Mani by kidnappers who'd sold him into slavery. He was aboard the *Amistad*, the second slave ship in a journey of wretchedness and pain. He was packed in a hold with fifty-three other Africans, many of them from his Mende tribe, but from other tribes as well. The crying and moaning came in Temne,

Sherbro, Kissi, Fula, Lokko, Ibo, Mandinka. It was June 29, 1839, and the *Amistad* was being thrown about in the turbulent waters off the coast of Cuba. They had been only three days out of port, but the storm that raged around them pushed the ship, its crew, and cargo farther and farther off course.

Since his abduction, Cinque had been engaged in an ongoing fight to keep from drowning in the vile effort to turn him into a piece of property. He was chained and tightly packed into a small two-masted schooner outfitted for carrying slaves from Havana to various locales. The *Amistad* was headed for Puerto Principe down the coast of Cuba. He would probably be sold as a field-worker in the sugarcane fields there. He was bound to live the rest of his life that way, in service to his white master. But he was fighting it with everything he had. And it *was* like drowning. A descent into an abyss of misery. Of having so many unknown and unanticipated things happen to you at one time that it was hard to remember who you had been. He held on to his wife's image in his head. He remembered the sound of his children as they played in the yard. He would not forget. He would do what he had to do to try to get back to them.

And so as he lay in his narrow space in the slave decks of the *Amistad*, as he had done nearly every minute since his capture, he thought desperately about ways of escape. Of finding a way out. He'd seen people kill themselves to keep from becoming slaves. He didn't want to die that way. But he would not resign himself either. He'd seen that, too. People who just got so tired of fighting the cruelty and violence that they gave up. And then they let other people decide for them who they were. That would not be him either. If he died, it would be while trying to escape. No one really knew, but Cinque, regardless of the chains and the distance he was from his homeland, was determined to return there.

The *Amistad* got underway from Havana within a day after the Africans and other cargo had been hastily loaded in. There were other ships in port awaiting their portion of the Africans who'd come in on the *Tecora*.

The *Tecora*. That had been the ship in which Cinque and more than seven hundred other Africans had been enchained for the journey from Africa. The "middle passage" it was called. It had been a monstrous, heartbreaking journey. Death and violence, starvation, beatings, disease, and mass murder swirled around them all the time. It took a strong constitution to survive the middle passage.

But survive he had. Along with hundreds of others. Then at four hundred fifty dollars a head, fifty-four of them had been purchased and marched aboard the *Amistad*, owned and captained by Ramon Ferrer and chartered by the "owners" of the cargo, José Ruiz and Pedro Montes.

The two Spaniards were taking their valuable human cargo and other supplies back home to Principe, some three hundred miles away. There, Cinque and the others would work their fields, cook their food, and raise their children. It was a trip that was expected to take between three and four days, depending on the wind.

On the second day out, sailing not far from shore and following the coastline, a sudden and ferocious storm had wrapped its strong arms around the *Amistad* and flung it to and fro like a child's toy. The rains pelted the ship and the wind whipped it about. The captain had, given the cargo he carried, tried to stay close enough to land so that no American patrol ships would hinder their journey. But the storm was so strong that it had steadily pushed the ship farther into the open sea.

One consequence of the ship's going off course was that the voyage was lengthened considerably. The success of any voyage depended on the ability of the captain to anticipate the length of the trip. All stores had to be laid in quantities to sustain both crew and human cargo until they reached their destination. Miscalculations could be devastating. So it was a critical decision when Captain Ferrer decided not to put into port to take on added supplies, thinking that the storm would abate and they would be able to make Principe within the estimated three or four days.

Such a decision meant that each of the Africans would suffer. That first day they were allotted only one banana, two potatoes, and a small cup of water. This was meager portion after the treatment they had received at the Havana *barracoons* where food had been plentiful. Havana was where the Africans who had survived the voyage to the new world could recover their health, and their value as well.

The small two-masted schooner bucked and twisted. It geed and yawed. Traveled the deep canyons the ocean created for them. Scaled the horrifying heights of angry water. There was very little ventilation in the slave hold and the heat was absolutely stifling. There were people heaving all around Cinque. He began to feel a little queasy himself. He fought with everything he had to keep his wits about him.

Against the noise of the wind and rough sea, the captives of the belowdecks resumed their customary communion with spirits. Yamba, the Temne, was chained across from Cinque. Yamba was still in great pain from a flogging he'd suffered at the orders of the captain. Fala, the Kissi with the pointed teeth, was near. Buakei and Gilabau, fellow Mende a little farther aft.

But the sound and fury of the weather seemed

to permeate every nook and cranny of the slave deck. There was a moment when Cinque could clearly hear the ship moan.

Yamba's beating had come earlier in the day, before the storm hit them, when some of the Africans had been allowed topside to stretch and take their turns at the water trough. He had taken more than his share. Captain Ferrer had caught him and ordered him flogged mercilessly. Cinque could see the pain on the Temne's face. The last African you would want to anger would be a Temne. But then, there was pain and anger everywhere. It always came back to one thing: escape.

He still had the faded and increasingly ragged charm his wife had made for him. He'd managed to it keep during the fight when he was kidnapped. He'd kept it during the long march through the heat and rain from Mani to Lomboko where they were loaded on the *Tecora*. He'd held it tightly every day. Whenever he needed inspiration, strength, he'd reach for it.

Unconsciously, he went for it now. It was wedged between his legs. He held it in his hand. He smelled her breath on his face. Felt her soft hand. He could see the deep blue of her favorite calico. The ship climbed a wall of water and then abruptly began a quick drop to the false bottom. There was a moment in the cycle of rising and falling that felt as if there were no limits. As if the water had no end. The ship would take its dive

16

into the trough of a wave with a confidence that was without reason.

Cinque's stomach lurched as the ship came to rest for a moment, waiting to be thrown upward again. Instinctively, he tried to steady himself against the movement of the ship. When he did, he accidentally dropped the charm, and for a moment he panicked. And then, feeling around with his hands, he thought he had found it. But what he felt wasn't a charm at all. It was a nail from a plank of the deck. It hadn't been driven all the way in. Or maybe someone else on a previous voyage had started dislodging it. There was just enough length at the head to begin working it out of the wood.

He hid the charm and began pulling and maneuvering the nail. He didn't know exactly what he was going to do with it, but it was the closest thing to a weapon he'd touched since he'd left Mendeland. He thought that maybe the nail would help him break free of the chains that held him down. He kept working it, trying desperately to pull it out.

Outside the lightning skipped, wires of light strung across the dark and rainy sky. The thunder didn't take long to sound its name on the heels of the lightning. Cinque wriggled the nail back and forth. There was virtually no light where he worked. He worked solely by feel. And as he pulled and jiggled and wriggled the nail, he could feel the skin on his fingers tear.

Even though shadows prevailed over all in the slave decks, there were eyes focused on him. Yamba stared. Shule, the elder, watched. Buakei strained against his chains. Across the gulf of culture and languages, the Africans, one by one, understood that something important was happening.

Cinque could now hear the muffled, anxious Spanish voices coming from above. He could tell that they were nervous. The stormy weather had seemed to be abating for a minute and then suddenly it kicked up again. The ship rattled like a child's toy with a broken piece shaking inside it. He worked harder at the nail. Now was the time to seek his freedom. The ship felt as though it might be torn apart. And, if the ship were to go down, if he couldn't find something to open the chains, they would all drown anyway. It was then it came to him. He would try to use the nail to open the manacles that held him down.

As he tugged and twisted at the nail, he heard them running overhead trying to secure the ship. Finally the timber gave way and the nail slipped out. He immediately jammed it into the keyhole of the manacle around his neck. A voice in his head pushed him forward. "Free. Get Free."

The nail tripped the latch and suddenly the manacle popped open and fell to the deck.

Cinque was stunned. It had been much easier than he'd ever imagined. All of that iron, held together by such a flimsy lock. For a second he realized how much their imprisonment depended on how hopeless they felt. All it had taken was the will to break free. But now, now the chains would be removed. He undid his cuffs and the connecting chains. Then he undid Yamba's and together they undid the rest. In no time the entire slave deck was free. The weight suddenly was gone. He touched his neck. He could feel the bruises raised like rope around his neck.

As the chains hit the wooden deck, Cinque saw heads pop up like sea birds reaching through the surf to find air before plunging back into the depths in search of fish.

"What now?"

"What should we do?"

"We must kill them and take this boat and go back home. They must die for what they've done." Cinque realized it was he who would have to lead them. He was prepared to die. He wanted to die if he wasn't to see home again. Behind him were the men, women, and children, late of Africa, and their anger was rising. Cinque could feel it all around him.

He took in a lungful of the stale air of the slave decks. He would never return to this life below if he could help it. He listened to the racket just outside the hatchway. It sounded like the Spaniards and their crew were frantic in their efforts to control the ship in the storm.

"We must find something to fight with. Follow me."

And then Cinque quickly pushed the hatch open and leaped onto the main deck. He stood there, his blood pounding in his heart, in his head.

Out of the corner of his eye, Cinque saw one of the Spanish crew coming toward him. The man looked as if he was about to scream, but Cinque wheeled around and grabbed him by the throat, choking off all but the slightest of sounds. Cinque then pushed him back a step and swung his fist at the man who was shocked that a slave would come at him that way. Cinque's blow found the sailor's head and knocked him backward. He lost his balance and Cinque was on him again.

In the confusion, the crewman lost his cutlass. Cinque watched it hit the deck with a muffled clank. He quickly reached down and retrieved it. He stared into the man's face. It was full of questions. But Cinque carried the anger from each day of his captivity in his arms and now it was in the blade he'd picked up from the deck. He watched as the man tried to gather himself in preparation for another attack and without any more reflection, Cinque ran him through. He felt the cutlass penetrate the man's chest and exit through his back finding air and wood on the other side.

Blood gushed forth from the man's chest and splattered the worn wood of the *Amistad.* It ran along the deck boards, thick and bright, mixed with the water from the swirling rain and began to flow across the ship. It stained Cinque's feet as he turned and waved those standing by the hatch to come forth.

And then, suddenly, his compatriots came issuing from the hold, their rage a part of the storm that visited the *Amistad.* This ship would now have to withstand not only nature's fury, but also that of black people who had lived, at the very least, the last four months in chains. The chains were now belowdecks and lay there like dead snakes.

Cinque made his way through the throng, entreating them to follow, and ended up in front of a locked storeroom. "There are knives in there. Maybe guns, too." He slammed the lock with the butt of his cutlass and it gave way.

Just inside the door there was a rack of cane knives. There were at least a hundred of them there. The line of Africans passing through to pick up weapons was steady. And then they were off again. Seeking to purge the ship of all its evil. Hoping to embrace Cinque's desire to take control and return themselves home.

The specter of bondage was enough to make the people angry enough to kill, but the ship's cook, Celestino, had also spurred anxiety in the

Africans when he made a not-so-subtle gesture
with his meat cleaver when they passed him as
they were being led to the slave decks. The Creole
cook had suggested that they would eventually
be turned into food and eaten. And everyone, but
especially the Kissi, Fala, was intent on avoiding
such an outcome. They really had no idea what
lay ahead for them under the domination of the
two Spanish merchants, but if it was about being
eaten by white people, they would fight to the
death.

Screams and trauma ricocheted throughout the
ship. Cinque knew that they were much more
likely to survive the night if they could take complete control of it.

Take control and sail it home.

There was pure disorder and riot erupting
everywhere. The Africans were running all about,
screaming, confronting other crew members as
they stumbled on deck, confused and startled by
the sound of the turmoil.

The fighting on deck and throughout the ship
was fierce. Blood gushed all around as the storm
battered them all. Cinque watched as one Spaniard screamed at another to warn him of Yamba's
approach, but the man didn't have enough time
to react and managed only to turn and face the
advancing African. Yamba, armed with the razor-
sharp, machetelike blade of the cane knife, cut
him down without hesitation. A small wave of

black people flowed around him as they moved toward the forecastle.

The crew undertook to defend themselves. It was clear that there would be no mercy, as was generally true when slaves threw off their chains. There is no fury like the rage of an ex-slave. And little soothes the experience of slavery. Certainly not the promise of life.

In front of Cinque, who now moved toward the bow, was a melee in which he watched one of the sailors strike down Foloma, one of the Temne, his stomach opening up like an overripe fruit, his essence spilling onto the deck. Cinque winced as he heard a scream which called the spirits and then watched the life fly out of the man's eyes.

And with that he let go the pent-up fury, the anger that had been growing in him since that day in his village—that day when his future was consigned to the dark stench-ridden hovels of subservience. Bondage. He took this fury and aimed it at the *Amistad* and its crew, as did every other black soul aboard. In groups they sought out anything moving as they raced across the ship.

Cinque strode directly into the sailor's line of vision, into striking distance, and brought his cutlass across his throat in one motion. The man stared at him, his life slowly fading, draining out of him at the neck. Cinque pushed his lifeless, dripping body down. He then turned to look at

Foloma and let out a brief sad sigh. He reached down and picked up the sailor's saber. Now he paraded about the ship with a cutlass in one hand, a saber in the other.

Cinque then came upon the ship's cook, the Creole who had suggested that Fala and the others would be eaten. And at just about the same time Fala appeared. The little warrior smiled at Cinque and looked at Celestino. Fala glowed in the flame of battle. He was a true warrior. Though small, he had obviously dreamed of this moment and seemed, to Cinque at least, to wear an expression of satisfaction.

The cook held his cleaver poised in the air near his shoulder. His gaze would not stop moving from face to face, trying to see who would come at him first. But Fala, not more than half the young man's height, in the blink of an eye, sliced his knife through the air. It passed by the cook's face like a spark and was back at Fala's side. He stood there smiling, a moonlit glint flashing from his teeth. For just a second all those standing nearby wondered what had happened, and then the cook's hand, still holding the cleaver, dropped to the deck. Thick warm blood flowed now where the wrist had been. And then Fala set upon him with his cane knife. Cinque watched as Fala ended any chance that the cook would ever threaten another African with being eaten.

There was another commotion amidships near

the lifeboats which drew Cinque's attention. He turned and ran in that direction. He saw two of the ship's crew making great haste toward a boat. He also saw Ferrer and his cabin boy, Antonio, darting about the deck, trying to avoid detection while trying to join their mates. But before the two could reach safety, three Africans appeared in front of them and blocked their advance.

Ferrer did not hesitate. He screamed and unleashed his saber in a grand stroke, immediately wounding one African in the measure. He took no pause before his saber struck the second. All the time he pressed toward the lifeboat. But Cinque had taken up position there. The captain, least of all, would escape his punishment.

Cinque stood there, Ferrer's worst dream: a saber in one hand, a cutlass in the other. Stripped of all clothes above the waist. Scarred and bleeding. Sweating.

Ferrer brought his saber up in a challenge. Instinctively, Cinque did the same. For an instant their swords crossed as if it were to be a civilized duel, over a matter of propriety or perhaps the love of a woman. The iron clashed among the roaring sounds of revolt which whistled about the ship. Captain Ferrer swung his cutlass wildly as if a sweeping pass would catch Cinque off guard. But the African was very agile and sidestepped the blow, delivering his own in the same instant. The captain fell, mortally wounded.

Cinque looked down on the fallen man. Ferrer opened his mouth and began to pray, to plead. "Please. Spare me. Please. I'm sorry. If you let me live, I will give you anything. Do anything. Please. I have a family. I'm sorry. Please."

Cinque heard the words as sobs and whines. He couldn't understand what Ferrer was saying and he didn't care. No one had cared when he had pleaded and sobbed. He stared into Ferrer's face and told him with his eyes, "You must pay for what you've done."

And then he drove his saber straight into the man's chest. He watched the light go out in Ferrer's eyes. For a moment Cinque wondered why he had wanted so badly to kill him. What exactly was it that Ferrer had done to him? But he had watched Ferrer flog many of the Africans, including the brutal beating of Yamba for supposedly stealing water.

And then he remembered those sick Africans on the *Tecora* standing together, waiting for that captain to send them to the depths. He wondered what they must have felt as their lungs filled with water, as they saw the approaching sharks. And what of their futures as spirits? What kind of afterlife was there underwater?

It took a particular type of person to buy and sell human beings. You almost *had* to see them as animals in order to sleep at night. In Cinque's mind, they deserved no mercy because they showed no mercy.

The racket abovedecks pulled both José Ruiz and Pedro Montes out of their sleep at precisely the same instant. They heard the thunder of bare feet on the wooden deck above them splashing and thudding in the blood and rainwater; the shouts in all manner of languages that careened from stem to stern. They met at the foot of the ladder which led amidships. They listened intently, trying to figure out what the commotion was all about, though there were enough agonizing screams to lend credence to their worst fears.

Without speaking, they crept up to the main deck. Chaos swirled there. They looked at each other and realized they were in serious trouble. It was so dark and there were so many dark bodies darting about.

Ruiz took a deep breath and headed toward the loudest commotion. Montes followed quickly behind him. They fast came upon Cinque standing over Ferrer. Ruiz motioned Montes back and they retreated into the shadows. But they heard the captain's pleas. And they saw Cinque advance on him. They also heard a number of Africans by Celestino hacking his body with the cook's own meat cleaver.

"We have to do something," Montes whispered to his associate. He drew his knife and ran to join another sailor who was fighting off a small group of Africans behind the foresail. Ruiz stood near the galley, shouting at the other Africans, hoping to scare them back into the hold.

The burden of slaver and slave master was in the folly of the privilege itself. No one commands other men indefinitely. When the slaves are in chains and must suffer cruelty, short rations, and inhuman conditions, they will cower at the sound of the voice of their master. But when the chains are broken, the sound of the slave master's voice is a call to arms.

And so it was. The first group advanced on Montes and beat him down with sticks and cane knives, though he was not killed. In the end, he staggered away, a deep gash above his ear and bleeding in various places. He crawled through the darkness and ended up behind a food barrel. There he pulled a sail over himself hoping to escape any more punishment.

Ruiz and Antonio, the cabin boy, were quickly captured by the Africans after suffering only minor wounds.

Cinque watched two crewmen run toward the lifeboats. They had paused there stricken as they witnessed Cinque kill Captain Ferrer. In their fear they then climbed into the lifeboats and began hacking furiously at the lines which held them aloft, over the water, trying to free themselves.

Cinque watched as the last rope was cut through and the boat slammed into the water, immediately becoming a part of the heaving Caribbean. The rain came in a torrent and the boat slowly began to angle away from the ship. But when the boat had hit the sea, it had opened a crack in its weathered hull. It almost immediately began taking on water. The ship was lined with Africans screaming at the escapees and pelting them with whatever they could pry loose from the deck.

For a second, Cinque thought about diving into the roiling sea to stop them himself, but before he could move, the boat dipped too deeply into the water at its bow and was now too heavy to maneuver. It quickly listed and took on more water and within a minute, as it slipped out of the reach of the ship, it began its descent to the bottom with the two crewmen screaming for help.

And then, there were no voices coming from the water and no boat to watch. They had disappeared. After only a matter of minutes, the mutiny was over. Cinque, Buakei, and Yamba were now in command.

Then the singing began as the Africans broke open every crate, smashed every closed door, pried open every cupboard in search of all the things they had been denied.

Are you all ready to go home?
The white man's witchcraft is strong.

It is time for us to rise up, rise up.
Toduy is the day
To face the wall

And occupy all the corners.
Do you want to go home?
Let's go.

Hey, get up people.
Today is a day to be remembered.
It will be a loss if you miss this day.

They found clothes and bolts of silk and other cloth. Rum and tobacco, medicines, and food stores. They began a night of revelry and celebration that transformed the ship from a floating mausoleum into a bustling, vibrant, even chaotic manifestation of nationhood. Suddenly those who were naked wore red pantaloons and yellow blouses. Some put on hats. Some stumbled about the deck still naked, but smiling.

Cinque had asked Buakei to watch after the three young girls to make sure they were safe. The night ended in the light moans of the wounded and the sighs of those who did not have to sleep with iron for the first time in four months.

2
By the Sun

*"One should not trust a crook on the strength
of his neat appearance."*

The first splash of light found the main deck crowded with tired, delirious Africans. Most of the dead had been thrown overboard, but the deck boards were covered in a sticky, greasy film of blood and debris. Everywhere you looked there was a bloody footprint or handprint, a splash of red drying in the new-day sun with hair protruding, or flecks of skin embedded.

Cinque had ordered Jose Ruiz bound down and held astern, where he had spent the night wondering if he would see light. Yamba and a few Temne had searched for Montes until they tired, and were now just stirring again. Cinque shook himself from sleep as well. He ended up slumped alongside the mainmast, exhausted and exhilarated. They'd managed to do it. They were free.

Suddenly there were shouts coming from starboard.

Montes had been discovered hiding under a canvas cover and dragged bleeding and begging aft to join his partner.

Meanwhile, as other Africans awoke on the ship, they renewed the search and exploration of their new domain. There were more cubbyholes and storage compartments to investigate.

Cinque slowly made his way aft. He approached the two captives. Now they were at his mercy. He could see the fear that stained the eyes of both men. Did they understand how angry he was? Did they know that he had prayed many times to have this opportunity? Actually as he looked at them, the picture of evil to him, he could tell that they did indeed know what Cinque was thinking. He saw them look at each other, trying to figure out what to do.

Montes carried more wounds than Ruiz, but the both of them seemed to be holding up better than one might expect after the night they'd had.

"We are in for it," Ruiz whispered to Montes. Montes nodded weakly.

Cinque stood over them. He fully intended to do to them what he had done to the captain. How dare they think him not capable of vengeance?

Ruiz took a long look at Cinque. Such an impressive figure, powerful and menacing. He could tell just from the African's countenance that he was bent on murder.

It was then that Yamba joined Cinque. "What

should we do with these animals? I feel like they should die like the others," Cinque said.

"Wait a little. This is a new day."

"No. These people are evil. They've beaten us. Starved us." Cinque spoke in hushed voice. He knew the two white men didn't understand him, but there was something about the deliberation of guilt and punishment which forced his voice low.

Yamba seemed unexpectedly pensive. "What you say is correct. But remember that we are in a strange land. We cannot speak their language. We are in a boat which is very different from our boats at home. If you kill them, we will be lost and drown out there," he said, pointing to the ocean which held them at its mercy.

Cinque thought for a moment and then responded, "But what has happened to us? Eh? We were captured and sold as slaves. White people are very cunning. If they get the chance, they will seize us again as slaves and we will be punished more severely."

Yamba considered Cinque's point. It was a good one. Yes, their only experience with white people was one of violence and cruelty. Still, how were they to get home? "The only way out now is to spare them and make them sail us back home."

Cinque shook his head. "Let me tell you again that the witchcraft of the white man is great. They sail over the great seas and capture slaves and bring them here to work for them. How will you know if they are sailing us back home? I feel we should kill them now."

"What you say is true, Cinque, but if we kill them, we will die also. If we spare them, whatever trick they play, we will still be alive."

"No." Cinque wanted Yamba to know that he'd not come this far to fall back into the power of white men. "As for me, I prefer to die than to be alive and in captivity as a slave."

Yamba broke from Cinque and turned to the two Spaniards, still speaking Temne. "You white men, do you promise to take us back to our home country in the east if we spare your lives?" He raised his arms to the eastern horizon. He stared first at Ruiz, and then Montes. They looked at each other.

Ruiz nodded slightly in the direction of Yamba. "That one wants us to sail them back." Ruiz, though incapable of understanding the language of the two Africans, nonetheless felt confident of his translation. He then turned his eyes to Cinque. "That one wants to kill us. He thinks he can sail all the way back without us."

Montes nodded his head. He agreed that whatever they were talking about had to do with his life and where they were going. Certainly he realized the predicament they were in. He'd heard accounts of mutinies before and knew that his life wasn't worth very much. But these were slaves, weren't they? And as mutinies went, this had been a rather bloody affair precisely for that reason. But these slaves had no facility with the ship, the sea, or the science of sailing, did they?

"Do you know how to sail this ship?" he whispered carefully, all the time staring at Cinque and Yamba debating their fate.

Ruiz considered the question for a moment and began to get the point, but before he could respond, he noticed Fala approaching. Of all the captives, Fala had always scared him the most. He wasn't even sure why he had purchased him. Those teeth. Ruiz shuddered.

"What's this?" Ruiz said more to himself than to Montes. But Fala was obviously sizing them up. Ruiz felt Montes's fear, too.

Fala smiled. It was as though he knew exactly how to frighten them.

Yamba spoke again. "We don't know what to do with you people. Either kill you or let you live. We want you to take us back home. But if you don't, we will kill you both."

Cinque relented. He didn't enjoy killing. If Yamba thought he could frighten the white men into helping them get back home, he was willing to go along.

Fala stood in front of Montes and Ruiz, motionless with a sinister grin on his face for a few moments, and then moved even closer when Cinque and Yamba broke from their conference.

Ruiz tried to look into Cinque's face. This one he also feared. Perhaps even more than Fala. Fala was a warrior. He was capable of great violence, but Ruiz understood the nature of warriors. But Cinque—Cinque was angry. Not a natural fighter. It was obvious that he came from privilege and the peace that that brought. But now, staring at him, Ruiz could see that Cinque's anger was more intense than anyone else's there.

Cinque put his face close to Ruiz and Montes and said, "Don't do any stupid thing if you don't want us to slit your fat white necks."

It didn't matter that the two Spaniards knew no Mende. Perhaps that was best anyway. Cinque wanted to kill them. Simple and to the point. Kill them and turn the ship in the opposite direction, back to Africa. It seemed the only sure way of ensuring that they would never be slaves again. Kill them both. But Yamba had convinced him that it was wiser to keep them alive if they helped guide the ship back to Africa.

"You must take us home or you will die," Cinque said to them. He then stepped back and raised his saber to the rising sun.

Ruiz now was confirmed in his suspicions. "Yes. East. To the sun." He said, but of course Cinque spoke no Spanish.

The African took his saber and brought it to Ruiz's manacled neck. There was no mistaking this gesture. He uncovered the bright whites of his eyes for Ruiz. They bored into him. He felt the threat in the touch of the blade, in the glare of Cinque's stare.

"I understand. You can trust me." He could speak only his language, and adjust his posture so that Cinque might know what he meant.

Cinque then motioned the saber toward the helm. Ruiz nodded and took hold of it, his chains rattling and dragging on the deck as he assumed control of the ship. He had no idea what was the right thing for him to do. At the moment though, it was clear that cooperation was essential to staying alive.

Ruiz straightened himself and turned the wheel. The rudder responded and slowly the ship began to turn eastward. "To Africa!" he shouted.

Cinque looked at the sun. For the first time in a long time he felt good. Free. He held his sword up and to the east.

And thus began the new voyage. The trip home. Sailing east by the sun to Africa.

3
Adrift

*"If you see that the sky has disappeared, what sense is
there in asking about where the stars would sit?"*

From the very moment of their liberation, the Africans began to redefine their lives. They marked off territory by tribe on the main deck and used colored sticks as lines of demarcation. The Kono. The Lokkos. The Sherbro. The Mende. The Temne. There were forty-one of them still alive. And that very first full night of freedom was spent in a restful and satiated euphoria.

There was plenty of food and water they thought, not knowing how long they were committed to being out to sea. There were no chains and no masters. No flogging and no maltreatment. And if they missed the sound of chains on human flesh, they could walk astern to the helm and watch Pedro Montes and José Ruiz deal with their own imprisonment. Or, on the forecastle, there was Antonio, chained to the anchor.

Cinque was amidships, standing by the main-

mast, holding on to a halyard. His imposing sil-
houette struck the pose of the many pirates who
had sailed these very same seas of the Spanish
Main.

What a world this was. Floating upon water in
a wooden structure. Being moved by the wind.
Buffeted by the rain. He had no idea how long it
would take to get them back home. He hardly
knew where home was now. But if they could be
brought all this way, then it must be possible to
find their way back. That's what he had pledged.
To Yamba. To everyone. He would not rest until
they were home.

He stared up at the sky. Unlike the night before, it was calm, hot, still, and the stars were
gemstones in the dark. He took a long breath. He
let the tension of the battle rise out of his body.
He had killed to feel like this. As he watched the
stars, he thought about his family. He felt for the
charm. It was still in the waist of his pants. The
sky above him was the same sky that was above
his family and his village. He would never forget
that. One sky.

And then, suddenly, it seemed the stars were
spinning around. He felt something shift in the
way the breeze hit his face. The wind seemed to
kiss the sails with new vigor. Cinque was disturbed, but couldn't tell what it was that bothered
him.

He stretched, paused, looked about the ship,

and headed to the stern. Ruiz was at the helm. Montes was asleep. There were two guards assigned there. They were Temne. Yamba had taken care of making the necessary arrangements for the guarding of the Spaniards. He noticed that Ruiz purposely did not look at him.

How could he not acknowledge me? Cinque thought. *I'm the one with the sword. This is our ship now. What is going on?* Cinque walked up to Ruiz, who seemed even more concerned with his heading and the response of the helm.

Cinque now stood next to him, his gaze fixed on the delicate skin of the ocean under the flattering light of the moon.

"What are you doing?" Cinque couldn't control himself. He knew Ruiz didn't understand Mende, and he himself understood no Spanish. But Cinque would not let that stop him from exerting influence, power over Ruiz. "Are you doing as you promised? We aren't going east now, are we?"

"What?"

"It seemed to me that the stars have changed positions. Are we still going in the right direction?" Cinque pointed his saber up at the stars.

All of this made Ruiz very nervous. He was a little surprised that Cinque had become suspicious so quickly. It frightened him. The only way to survive this deception was to stay committed to it. He had to convince Cinque that he could be trusted. And the one power Ruiz held over all the Africans was their belief that he knew how to sail the ship, a skill of which they knew nothing.

He and Montes had a plan, but it wouldn't even have a chance of success if this deception didn't work. He looked at Cinque and nodded tentatively. He was busy thinking of the right tactic to take with Cinque. He knew he was playing with fire. Cinque seemed capable of anything.

Cinque walked to the navigation table and looked at the maps. He then looked at the compass, trying to understand in an instant what he couldn't know. The sea was its own territory. Its own world. What magic would help a man guide such a vessel across the vast water? He looked at Ruiz and wondered if even he knew the sea well enough to control the fate of the *Amistad* and its inhabitants. But certainly Cinque, who had seen a ship and then the ocean for the first time less than a year ago, would never be able to read the maps and understand from the ship's heading what Ruiz was doing.

Still, he could try to get Ruiz to reveal any plot that might be in the works by simply scrutinizing his actions carefully. Try to keep the Spaniard off balance. How could Ruiz know what Cinque knew or didn't know? Indeed, Cinque was quite sure that Ruiz would underestimate him at every turn.

"Well, I have to tack, don't I? Tack. You'd rather

I didn't? Do you want to get there? I have to tack," Ruiz said quickly and looked away. He could feel Cinque's eyes on him. He had to keep a steady head.

Cinque took another long look at the navigational equipment and maps and another at Ruiz, now catching the man's gaze. He threatened him without uttering a word. Ruiz felt it, and knew then that Cinque might kill him at any moment if he should uncover his betrayal.

And then Ruiz struck on a masterful ploy to get Cinque off his back. He let go of the wheel. It began spinning, slowly at first, and then as it picked up momentum, it went quickly out of control. The compass began to gyrate. Now the sky above them twirled like a picture on a pinwheel.

"Here, you sail it. You want to sail it? Here."

Cinque grabbed the wheel just as Montes, who had been sleeping against a wall was moved by the force of the turning ship and hit his head. He jolted awake and stared at the image of Cinque at the helm.

And it was a powerful image indeed. Cinque himself felt it. He had to admit that he felt the power in his hands and was instantly attracted to it. He looked at the compass as its frenetic movement slowed. He could see how his own strength was transferred to that of the ship. The stars had stopped spinning, and suddenly the sails were re-invigorated and filled with wind.

Ruiz looked at Montes. They hadn't counted on this. If Cinque realized that he could sail the ship, there would be no reason to keep them alive.

Ruiz reinserted himself at the helm, using a tone of voice which was intended to make Cinque think he was doing something wrong. "Give me the wheel. You're going to get us all killed." Ruiz couldn't believe his own courage. But if he couldn't convince Cinque that only he could truly command the helm, all was lost. He took back control of the wheel.

Cinque turned to him, unsure of what was going on. "I've warned you," he said in Mende, pointing again at the stars. "Don't do anything stupid."

"Right. Whatever you say. You can count on me. Now get out of here," Ruiz responded in Spanish.

Cinque walked away from the helm. He hoped he had convinced Ruiz to do as he had commanded.

After Cinque was some distance away, Ruiz relaxed with a smile and a relieved sigh. "That was close," he said to Montes.

"Yes, too close if you ask me."

"We have no choice. I have no intention of sailing this ship back to Africa."

* * *

Five days later they had sailed into what they thought was the vast expanse of the Atlantic Ocean. The spirits of the Africans was bright and excited. They were going home.

It didn't take long for most of the Africans to appropriate the clothes and accessories of the dead crew. They also raided their stores and lockers. The individual personalities of the newly freed began to bloom. Buakei, for example, now wore a scarf around his neck. It flapped in the ocean breeze as he walked about deck. Yamba had acquired a captain's hat, which he now wore all the time.

Cinque watched as Yamba held court with his Temne constituency. He had to admit that he didn't like Yamba. His arrogant and chauvinistic attitude about the superiority of the Temne aggravated Cinque. They were no better than the Mende.

Buakei interrupted his reflection. "Cinque, we are running out of food. There was very little stored. They were only expected to be at sea for two or three days. Our journey most likely will take weeks."

"I hadn't thought about that. I thought there was plenty of food."

"We haven't been frugal either. Maybe we've celebrated a little too much."

Cinque regarded the dilemma. He decided then that if they saw another ship, they would try to trade some of the goods they found on board for food and water. He also put Yamba on the lookout for any land mass where they might put to shore and fill the freshwater barrels.

It had been twenty days since they had taken control of the *Amistad*. Cinque and Yamba stared up at the sails and the stars, waiting for it to happen again. Every night the same thing. Suddenly the stars revolved again as the wind hit the sails, and the ship changed course again.

"Do you see?" Cinque whispered.

"Ah . . . you worry too much. We are going toward the rising sun. That's where home is."

"But something is wrong, Yamba."

"You are a farmer, Cinque. What do you know about the stars?"

"Farmers know more than you think they do."

Every night, when Ruiz and Montes were at the helm, they turned the *Amistad* around. The Africans were bound to the east in their search for Africa, and the Spaniards were committed to going west, trying to take the ship back to Cuba or failing that, to work their way to American shores. In a way, they were trying to go home, too. Every night the stars would seem to spin on an axis. What was fore became aft. What was port became starboard.

Ruiz and Montes were smart enough to make their adjustments late at night, when most of their passengers were asleep. But Cinque had seen enough to be suspicious. And he didn't know what to do with his suspicions. It was obvious that Yamba wasn't too concerned.

Many of the newly unshackled Africans now spent their days basking in the sun, drinking whatever alcohol could be found aboard ship, and eating. There was continuous singing. Occasional celebrations and prayers emanated from each of the various encampments about the main deck.

No one attended to the sails or the general fitness of the vessel. Ruiz and Montes had no interest in such concerns. They hoped they were drifting slowly back into Cuban waters.

Every day the ship was pointed east to the sun. And every night, whenever they figured it was safest, either Ruiz or Montes turned the ship west or northwest. For days Montes secretly used the islands of the Bahamas as a mark in his effort to keep the ship off course. And after more than a week of such maneuvering, he began to take the ship more northward. As a consequence, the *Amistad* made little progress in any particular direction.

Thirty days after he had taken control of the *Amistad*, Cinque sat on the periphery of the Mende encampment. There were Africans sprawled all about, trying to find a late night breeze, though there wasn't much of one. There was actually a low-level mist encircling them. And it seemed to be slowly but steadily thickening.

Over the past hour Cinque had been watching Buakei with a little amusement. Buakei was Mende and therefore spent most of his time near the main mast, where the Mende assembled. But farther aft were the Temne, Yamba's people. Among the Temne there was a young woman, a teenager, Maseray. Cinque had seen Buakei waving at her before. But the tribal way was strong aboard the *Amistad* and comingling was not encouraged. Besides, except for the three young girls that Montes had bought—and who were now kept isolated from the rest of the Africans in the captain's cabin—Maseray was the only woman on the *Amistad*.

Buakei had been inching himself closer and closer to the Temne camp. Eventually he gathered enough courage to cross over the sticks that marked the Mende boundary and resettled closer to the Temne's.

Yamba had also been watching Buakei. Part of his responsibility as the Temne leader was to protect Maseray as he had been doing since their liberation. He, too, was lightly entertained by the flirtatious activity between the young Mende and Maseray. But enough was enough. He walked over to Buakei and stared at him.

Buakei, who had been trying to get Maseray's

47

attention, looked up and found Yamba's eyes bearing down on him. Buakei instantly froze and then, as if jolted by some invisible bolt of lightning, began to scoot back into the Mende camp. He wanted no part of Yamba.

Cinque almost laughed out loud. Buakei was brave, but not foolish. It was then Cinque noticed the winking lights of what he thought might be a ship in the near distance. He squinted to see better through the fog. It was definitely a ship.

He jumped up and began running about deck, silencing the chanting tribes. Finally his voice rolled throughout the ship.

"Silence!" he commanded in Mende and slowly the ship became silent. There was creaking wood, the clang of metal against metal and of the halyards against the masts, but nothing else.

Cinque then grabbed a musket from a stash piled near the galley and headed astern. When he reached the helm, where both Ruiz and Montes were standing, he shoved them out of the way and reshackled them. He blew out the oil lamps and grabbed the helm.

Montes watched the African closely. He saw how his wide nose flared whenever there was trouble. He saw how fierce Cinque could be. In the dark, his blackness made him seem like a statue.

Montes whispered to Ruiz, "We have to signal them somehow."

"When the ship gets closer, even he will run and hide. Then we both start yelling." But even as he said this to Montes, Ruiz realized that if they were successful in attracting attention to the ship, it would most certainly be boarded and searched. This frightened him more than he wanted to admit. Transporting slaves was against the law and all of the evidence had not been destroyed back in Havana. "They'll search the ship."

Ruiz watched Cinque steer the ship while, at the same time, trying to see through the fog. There was definitely a ship approaching. But Ruiz took the opportunity to slip a flat leather pouch out from under the charts and push it through a crack to the deck below.

Cinque was so focused on trying to see the approaching vessel that he didn't see Ruiz hide the pouch. Cinque was more concerned with the potential of a collision. The ship continued to bear down on the *Amistad*. Everyone on deck could feel its presence grow as it came closer. And then its sounds joined those of the *Amistad*.

"Get ready," Ruiz whispered to Montes.

Cinque did, however, divert his attention just long enough to see Ruiz and Montes whispering to each other. He quickly figured that they were planning to try something. He quietly reached down and grabbed a rope and tied off the wheel so it would hold the rudder steady. He then picked up his musket. Ruiz and Montes were so busy talking in hushed voices that they didn't see Cinque approach.

They both waited with anticipation, hoping to soon see what ship was out there. They'd decided to shout bloody murder when it came into view.

But before they could begin shouting, Cinque crept up behind them and shoved the muzzle of the musket against Ruiz's head. Cinque saw the two men flash looks of surprise. Then they both simultaneously turned their heads to the helm. He knew he had beaten them to the punch once again. How long would they continue to underestimate him?

At first Ruiz closed his eyes and trembled at the thought of the musket discharging. But then he thought perhaps he was being a bit too cowardly. He took a deep breath and said to Montes, out of the side of his mouth, "What am I afraid of? He doesn't know how to use it."

At which precise moment, Cinque cocked the old musket, and put a finger to his lips. "Shhhh . . ." Both Montes and Ruiz were quite shocked. So much for assumptions when it came to Cinque. The African continued to amaze them. He had deduced the proper handling of the musket and had obviously learned the appropriate gestures one must use to shut people up.

The stillness was broken suddenly by the sound of a band playing. It was the "Blue Danube," a Viennese waltz, and it came from the other ship, which was now very close. Cinque watched as it came into view and passed within inches from the *Amistad*. Cinque could see a group of white figures on board, frozen in horror as they looked upon the *Amistad* with its crew of Africans dressed in all manner of styles, lounging about deck.

And then it was gone, disappearing into the fog, the music dissipating like light from a waning sun.

Over the next thirty days, the ship began a descent into the depths of stagnation that would frighten the saltiest of sailors. It was evident in the sounds or, more truthfully, in the lack thereof. Days aboard a ship that is vibrant and alive, with an active crew, are spent in the continuous process of the ship's work. Constant inspections and the resulting repair of vital shipboard necessities is routine: the mending of sails, the removal of barnacles from the hull, retarring surfaces, swabbing, and primping. This was the only way to keep a vessel shipshape. But of course the new commanders had no knowledge of such business and the ship suffered because of it.

Montes and Ruiz, who still managed the helm, further undermined the Africans by allowing the sails to flap in the wind, so that even during the day when Cinque and the others could monitor the direction they were going, the *Amistad* made little headway.

So instead of making its way across the Atlantic as Cinque and the others thought, they were actually drifting steadily north. They were snaking their way up the coast of the United States of America. For sixty days they had teetered back and forth. One day west, that night north and east, the next day west, the day after north and east. Occasionally Montes or Ruiz would sight a ship in the distance and would purposefully try to stay in a specific area, hoping that the ship would come back for a closer look. But none came.

And as the days passed, the supplies dwindled. The sails were now in such disrepair that they were virtually nonfunctional. And as the freshwater barrel drew closer and closer to empty, some of the Africans began to drink whatever liquids they had found among the ship's cargo and stores. Many were taken ill before it was discovered that some of them had been drinking liquids that were poisonous. Eight more men died during their voyage.

To be sure, there were other captains who saw the *Amistad* out at sea. But when the telescope was aimed at them, the image was too frightening. They saw what the other ship had seen: Black men wandering above decks with long knives, some with muskets, dressed in the elaborate and gaudy costumes they'd found among the captain's possessions.

There was a captain who accidentally passed close enough to the *Amistad* to deduce that they needed water and brought his ship alongside so that they could transfer a keg of water and some apples to the strange ship.

But Cinque became very nervous. He worried that Ruiz and Montes might cause a disturbance. He also couldn't stop himself from believing that the white captain on the other ship might try to board and take the *Amistad*. As a precaution, he ordered everyone to prepare to defend the ship.

The captain of the other ship saw Cinque and the others arming themselves, and immediately panicked. His crew had been anxious during the entire interaction. He feared that Cinque and his crew were pirates or worse still, ghosts. A *Dutchman* of bloodthirsty killers. He ordered the lines that held the two ships together cut and swiftly moved away.

This incident gave further credence to the rumors and stories of the ship and its passengers that had begun to circulate along the eastern seaboard of the United States. On their sixty-third day at sea since taking control of the *Amistad*, there was suddenly a shift in the winds of the moment.

On that day, Fala stood at the bow of the ship and stared out at the horizon. And there, through the mist was the outline of a distant shore which grew as the mist cleared and they got closer. At first Fala thought maybe he'd fallen asleep and was in a dream. And then he was sure. It was land. It was home. They were home.

"Home!" Fala screamed. "Home."

Cinque was close by, but facing aft. He'd been talking with Yamba about their lack of water. He walked over to where Fala was now jumping up and down and pointing. Others slowly began to take up the chant of "deliverance" and "home." But Cinque wasn't convinced. The Spaniards had tricked them. He was nearly sure of it.

He called Yamba over. "I don't think this is home."

"The stars again? You think they have fooled us, don't you?"

"I'm pretty sure of it. I think only some of us should go ashore. The rest should stay here until we return."

Yamba regarded Cinque. He was naturally the leader. His voice was the one most listened to. At first Yamba had thought Cinque to be nothing more than a tall farmer. Nothing special. But he had been watching and he could see how easy it was for Cinque to bark orders at everyone. People just seemed to want to follow him without question. Sometimes Yamba, too, found himself mindlessly going along with Cinque's wishes. After all, if it weren't for Cinque, they might never have gotten free. Still, Yamba wasn't comfortable letting the Mende have so much power over him and his people. It wasn't right.

"Yes. That's what we should do. We need to search for some fresh water anyway. I'll have a few of my people make a boat ready."

"I will come as well." It was Fala. The sun cast a glint on his sharpened teeth.

"Why should you come, Kissi? This is an adventure for big men." Cinque laughed. But Fala did not smile.

"Do you need me to show you what a big man can do?"

"No, Fala." Cinque put his hand on the shoulder of the young warrior. "I think it is a good idea that you come with us. Who knows what we will see there."

"Yes." Now Fala smiled. "Who knows?"

4
Captured

"People drown in rivers that do not
seem fearful to them."

It was a bright Saturday morning, the 26th of August when they rowed to shore in one of the lifeboats. There were Cinque, Buakei, Yamba, Fala, and two others, Kahleh and Ba, fully armed and with their senses sharply tuned.

"Bring the water barrel," Yamba whispered to Kahleh and Ba, who swung the barrel out of the boat and dragged it behind them. Cinque led them quickly up a ravine along the edge of a woods. There they quickly came to a stream of fresh water.

Fala saw the water first and ran to it. And after a tentative taste, he drank heavily from his cupped hands.

"It is good."

He was quickly joined by the others. After they were refreshed, Kahleh and Ba began filling the barrel from the stream.

Suddenly Cinque put his hand up to still their movements. They could all hear something clatter in the distance as it approached along a sloping dirt road which lay just a foot or two on the other side of a run of bushes. They crouched low. But one by one, they began rising again so they might see what was about to pass by them.

And then it was visible: It was a hobbyhorse bicycle with a black man riding it. They all stared at each other as the bicycle passed. Cinque watched the man turn back toward them. He could see the amazement on the face of the man.

Cinque motioned to the others and they retreated into the woods. "We'd better be careful." No one spoke of the two-wheeled contraption with the black man sitting atop it.

Yamba noticed a narrow path in the woods and pointed it out to Cinque. "We could go this way."

Cinque could see in everyone's face the desire to see more of the land they found themselves in. They headed off along the path. Soon, they came to a section where the woods thinned and allowed a view of a large driveway, which wound its way horseshoe fashion in front of a grand Colonial mansion. Cinque and the others huddled in an outcropping of trees at the foot of the driveway.

Through the leaves they could see a three-foot-high statue of a black man holding a lantern. Beside it was a large carriage with a real black man dressed in a colorful and, to them, obviously regal uniform. He was perched atop the carriage like a grand master.

In fact, everywhere the Africans looked, they saw others just like themselves. Only better dressed and scarless. There were house servants ducking in and out of the house. The liverymen and gardeners were busy about their tasks on the grounds of the estate.

Buakei pointed to the coachman, who seemed to sit more still than the statue below him. "He must be the big man here."

Cinque nodded, but the longer he watched the parade of people and the manner in which they went about their duties, the less certain he was that *any* of the black people could have been the "big man."

And then he saw a white woman emerge from the side of the house and approach two black women who were working in the garden. He had noticed the women before. They wore no marks or scars or indication of tribe or status, but seemed to be at peace cutting flowers and talking to each other. But when the white woman approached them, they underwent a sudden transformation.

Cinque watched as their demeanor changed. Suddenly their heads began to bow in deference. They seemed completely unwilling to make eye contact with the woman. To Cinque it seemed they danced a dance they seemed to know very well. He saw resignation in their eyes. This was what they were supposed to do. They were expected to demonstrate their inferior status to the white woman at every opportunity.

And then the truth of the situation was revealed to him. Perhaps this was what had been meant for them. To the side of the house, they had seen a black man who'd been saddling a horse. When Cinque looked in his direction, he could see the black man holding the reins as a young white man came out of the stables and climbed onto the horse.

It was a quick education. An older man strode out of the front door of the mansion. This, thought Cinque, this man is the "big man" here. And sure enough, as the man walked up to the carriage, the well-dressed black man snapped to attention and another black man, the footman, appeared with his head bowed in subservience and opened the coach door.

Cinque turned to Yamba. "Let's get out of here."

Together they made their way back to the path and then onto the beach where they had left their boat. Kahleh and Ba held up the rear, dragging the water barrel. They reemerged from the woods just in time to see a ship in full sail maneuver toward the *Amistad*.

It was the U.S.S. *Washington*, a Navy survey brig

which had been specifically ordered to hunt down the phantom "pirate ship." It was commanded by one Lieutenant Gedney, who ordered Lieutenant Meade to seize the schooner, its cargo, and the Africans. They'd been looking for the *Amistad* for a few days. There'd been reports up and down the coast and already the newspapers of Connecticut and New York were talking about a ghost ship.

Cinque and the others could see their countrymen on deck, obviously screaming at them to hurry back. The American flag that flew from the advancing ship provided background to the chaotic scene on the ship.

Cinque's stomach lurched. Suddenly everything was in jeopardy. He ran to the lifeboat and grabbed an oar. The others quickly followed. Together, they began a frenzied effort to row back to the *Amistad*.

As they pulled their way through the wake, Cinque saw two longboats lowered from the *Washington*. In them were men armed with muskets and pistols. He could see the guns protruding from the boat like remnant feathers from a plucked chicken. Cinque felt the tension rising as they raced the two naval boats to the *Amistad*. Fala jumped to the prow of the boat, produced his saber, and screamed a challenge at the top of his voice. Even as they plowed the water with their oars at a feverish pitch, the scream startled the sailors into a momentary hesitation. They could see this small figure standing like old Blackbeard himself at the head of the boat.

And to the surprise of the Africans in the boat, someone on the *Amistad* had made a decision to hoist the anchor. They could see two men heaving at the anchor line. As they pulled it aboard, the ship immediately began to move away as the wind took up what was left of the ragged sails.

When the ship began to move forward, those on the *Amistad* were suddenly tossed about. Ruiz, who was at the helm at the time, seized the opportunity and cracked his Temne guard on the head with the manacles on his wrists.

Cinque looked at Yamba, and then to the ship as it swung away from them. Fala screamed again, pointing out that the longboats had separated, one heading for the *Amistad*, the other for their boat.

Cinque could now hear Ruiz and Montes shouting in Spanish at the naval ship as they turned the *Amistad* in its direction. But there was no time to consider what Ruiz was doing, because the longboat was fast coming upon them. Fala hurled an oar like a spear into the chest of an American sailor.

The sailors began firing their muskets into the air. To them, Cinque and his clan were obviously pirates. The rumors of their adventure had preceded them. And now, faced with the little terror that Fala presented of himself, they were taking no chances.

At the first report of firearms, Cinque ordered them all into the water. His mind was set on swimming to the *Amistad*.

The sailors reloaded and fired again. Yamba slowed his strokes. He was no swimmer and neither were any of his people. Where were they going anyway? After the second round of shots, all of them stopped trying to swim—except Cinque, who ignored the warning shots and kept going.

Yamba, Buakei, Fala, Kahleh, and Ba struggled in the water as they looked into the muzzles of the guns trained on them. The second longboat was now aimed at Cinque, who was working his body furiously, trying to get to the *Amistad*. The sailors who pursued him doubled their effort, a bit surprised at his strength.

And, in truth, Cinque did not mean to be caught. He didn't know who was chasing him, but he did know that if they caught him he would find himself in chains again . . . or worse. He kicked harder. He would lead them home with him if they couldn't overtake him. In front of him the sun sat aloft and beckoned. Home was that way. That way. And Cinque swam, putting everything he had into his own freedom.

He went on like that for minutes, outkicking the rowers and their longboat. But they began to catch up. He could hear them chanting, "Heave. Heave." Someone else, someone at the back softly alternated, "Ho." It was a familiar cadence.

Cinque felt them a fathom away. And then in an instant he decided to take matters completely into his own hands. That was what freedom was anyway. He couldn't let them put him in chains again. He slipped under the surface, hoping to go down so deep he'd never come up.

He felt the sun on his back. His wife's voice sang a song she often sang at harvest time. It asked for a bountiful harvest. Her voice was full of life and anticipation. How long had he been gone? How far had he traveled, carrying the weight of iron on his back? Now, here he was sinking into the Atlantic. In a place that he had never even thought existed. Had never even imagined.

But her voice beckoned. Was he giving up? Was this giving up? He hadn't wanted to give up. He just wanted to be out of the grasp of everyone who had tied him down. That was a living death, entombed in the womb of the wooden world. The creaking, groaning death of the slave ship.

Her voice stayed with him. She wanted him back. He was her harvest. He would find his way home unless they stopped him. He couldn't do their work for them. He couldn't give up now, after he'd come so close.

And just as he began to lose the last of his held

AMISTAD

breath, he began to ascend. Like a fish, he moved to the light and broke through to the surface, where the sailors, leaning over to see him better, waited anxiously.

"Hey, mate, didn't think you had gills. Thought you'd have to get a little air sometime or 'nother. Come aboard." With that, Cinque was quickly and indelicately hauled out of the water.

5

New Haven

Lieutenant Gedney ordered that the *Amistad* be towed into the harbor of New Haven, Connecticut, where he sought to lay salvage claim to the ship and its cargo.

Popular excitement about the *Amistad* spread shortly after its arrival the following day. There were many diverse reports. Some labeled the Africans as pirates. Others extolled the bravery of Gedney and his crew. There were even opinions that the Africans had had every right to fight for their freedom.

Now the *Amistad* lay at anchor alongside the *Washington*. It was another bright late summer day. Lieutenant Gedney, a stern-faced, professional sailor strode across the plank that connected the two ships. He seemed unconcerned as a sailor standing on the *Amistad* spoke out clearly, "Make way for Lieutenant Gedney."

Once on the *Amistad*, he cast his gaze across its deck. He saw the Africans dressed in the tattered remnants of European clothes. There was a large pile of confiscated weapons, including sabers, muskets, and cane knives. There also was a tangle of American, British, Protuguese, French, and Spanish flags spilling from a crate. And, of course, the always-present leg irons, chains, and manacles strewn about the general confusion of the main deck.

He nodded to his subordinate, Lieutenant Meade. "Pirates, eh?"

But before Meade could respond, a commotion erupted from astern. Sailors approached, dragging the still manacled, bedraggled Ruiz and Montes along with them.

Cinque couldn't help but flash an I-told-you-so look at Yamba. Alive, the two Spaniards could only mean trouble for them. But, at the same time, they both found the situation just a bit humorous as Ruiz and Montes were literally crawling on the deck as they made grand appeals and gave great thanks for being rescued.

Gedney leaned into Meade. "Are these two begging for mercy or expressing their gratitude?"

Meade shrugged. As they began putting the picture together, it was quickly forming to the disadvantage of Ruiz and Montes. Neither of the two officers had any sympathy for slave traders.

And then a sailor emerged from the slave

decks. "Sir." He stood by the open hold hatch with a handkerchief over his mouth. Gedney and Meade deliberately approached the hold. Gedney kneeled down and peered into the darkness of the hold. It didn't take much time, nor did he have to venture inside, to know what he was dealing with. He stood up and turned to face the Africans. Then Ruiz. Then Montes. "I want them off this ship right away. Make whatever arrangements you need to."

"Aye, aye." And with that Lieutenant Meade turned and exited to the *Washington*.

"We should attack them." Fala was despondent, but ready to do battle.

"Attack them how, Fala? We are once again weighed down by iron." Yamba looked to the starboard side of the ship, and then out to the open water.

"I'm not afraid. If we—"

Cinque interrupted them with a slight movement of his head. "This is no time for hopelessness or idle threat. Maybe they will let us go home."

And then the sailors, just as the slavers had done months earlier, threaded a chain through their manacles and stood them up.

"It doesn't look like they are going to let us go anywhere, Cinque," Yamba whispered.

They were led into boats and taken to shore.

During the two months they had been at sea, Cinque had fervently believed that he would eventually prevail and find his way home. Even though he knew in his heart that they weren't going in the right direction, he never really expected to be recaptured. But now he had to face the reality that they were once again prisoners. He had to deal with the fact that he would not be going home anytime soon.

And so chained together, the Africans were escorted by Coast Guard and Navy sailors armed with loaded rifles and fixed bayonets. They were admonished to remain silent. The trip to shore was almost surreal. The Africans were about to take up temporary residence in their third country in one year. Twice as chattel and now as alleged criminals.

They were pulled out of the boat, officially setting foot in the United States of America. New Haven, Connecticut to be exact. 1839. The shroud of night was dropping around them. In front and around them, constables carried torches that lit their way. Amazement and surprise rippled among the captives as they were marched along the wharf and into the town. Citizens, black and white, stopped on the streets and stuck their heads out of windows in wonder. Excitement skipped along Chapel Street and swirled up and down the alleyways.

Their route up Chapel Street would take them

to the open area of the village green with its three church spires and the state house in the background.

They ended their march at a hugh stone building. The procession passed through the former stockade's iron-barred gates.

Two men observed the spectacle at a safe distance away from the crowd. They stood outside the tavern adjacent to the stockade. One of the men was Colonel Stanton Pendleton, the town's jailer. The other was the magistrate who had ordered their imprisonment, Andrew T. Judson.

Judson seemed satisfied that all had gone well and spoke with confidence, "We should be happy to discuss with you later, Colonel Pendleton, the exact financial arrangements."

"We'll discuss them now." Pendleton considered his position and couldn't help smiling at the situation. An unexpected forty bodies to house. Not to mention the three young girls, who had also been remanded into his custody. "Unless the mayor would prefer to board them at his house."

The magistrate grimaced and let out a sigh. He knew that the advantage was with the jailer. He could have asked for almost anything and probably gotten it.

The prisoners were now being herded into two large, adjoining cells. The girls were led across a large muddy courtyard and guided into a smaller cell. They were ultimately destined for Colonel Pendleton's house for safe keeping.

Cinque had been silent for the longest time. There wasn't much to say. He knew that no one among them could change their plight. Even Yamba was dejected. They were all tired and hungry and sad. But as he approached the cell, Cinque decided that this would be a good time to refuse. They'd all been pushed and pulled and told what to do. What if he just refused to go into his cell?

Which is what he did. He began backing up as he reached the cell door. But there was an instant response: One of the guards slammed him in the back with a baton. Fala, who was behind Cinque, jumped on the back of the guard who'd hit him. But two other guards peeled Fala from their comrade and threw both of the Africans into the cell and slammed it shut.

The sound of iron clanging had become familiar to Cinque. More than familiar. A kind of haunting. His chains were iron and their rattle had been with him since he'd been kidnapped. The sound of iron was the sound of restraint. Order. Domination.

6

Clarion Call

Seven thousand miles away, a pale, even gaunt, white nine-year-old girl sat at an extravagantly long table. A table that measured thirty paces from end to end, with twenty chairs on either side. As large as it was, it was stark in the room that was as massive and grand as any royal dining area. At various intervals around the cavernous room, servants stood awaiting whatever her whims dictated.

She was quite at home there at her large table, eating breakfast alone. This child was Isabella II, the reigning Queen of Spain, hoisted to power in 1833 by circumstances convoluted enough to have caused the Carlist wars and put the viability of an entire country under her dominion.

In a manner of some abruptness, her meal was interrupted by one of her naval officers. She heard his medals jangling on his chest as he approached. Then he stood, waiting for her acknowledgment. But she continued with her meal. Uninvited military men never brought good news. She already knew this. And besides, whatever was bothering him was probably of little concern to her.

The admiral cleared his throat. "Your Majesty. Something's happened."

Isabella continued eating. Even she was conscious of how loud her silverware sounded against the china plates.

Finally the young queen looked up.

"Your Majesty," he began again, "there has been an . . . ah . . . an incident. In American waters . . ."

Meanwhile, across the ocean, American president Martin Van Buren was at a very different point in his career. He stood on a well-decorated wagon, covered with red, white, and blue bunting and crepe. Flags and a banner which announced his intentions: REELECT VAN BUREN— GOD BLESS AMERICA. Around him the loud, bright music of a brass band boomed. The tuba and the trombone played tag with the drum and everything crackled with patriotic fervor.

His administration had faced all manner of troubles, almost from the very beginning. A financial panic had struck the nation. Bankers begged Van Buren for aid, but he blamed the bankers for the crisis and insisted that government manipulation would only further weaken the economic structure. Van Buren also inherited from his former boss, President Andrew Jackson, the Seminole Indian War in Florida—a conflict that was still claiming thousands of lives on both sides and costing the government tens of millions of dollars. One of Van Buren's strengths often worked against him. He was known to be extremely calm in the face of crisis and this angered people who thought a chief executive should be more expedient. But no concern was more fraught with dread than the growing worry over slavery and the drawing of lines by the Southern states against the charges of the Northern ones.

He was in Arlington, Virginia, working the hustings for votes as the campaign headed into the fall. It was late August, and his efforts to be reelected were facing rather stiff opposition. The country was already beginning to come apart at the seams. Still, he waved to various faces. Some he knew, most he didn't. He wanted to seem confident. In control. He felt Hammond's presence beside him before he was there. Leder Hammond was Van Buren's personal secretary.

"Mr. President, we've taken a ship into custody."

"What?" The noise around them was nearly deafening. Hammond was virtually screaming.

"A ship of blacks, sir."

The president smiled even more broadly for his constituents. "Who?"

"The Navy has taken a ship full of blacks, Africans I think, into custody. It's a Spanish ship, Mr. President."

The shadow of a frown passed over Van Buren's face. It wouldn't be until much later in the day, as they traveled over the Virginia countryside by train, that the matter would arise again.

The campaign was exhausting and he really wanted to relax for an hour or two with a snifter of his favorite brandy and a cigar. But he knew from Hammond that the Spanish emissary was already aboard the train and waiting for an audience.

"Send him in," the president said, with just a trace of agitation in his voice.

After the appropriate pleasantries were exchanged, Angel Calderon de la Barca, Spain's ambassador sat down across from Van Buren. "The schooner was conveying the slaves from Havana to Puerto Principe when the attack occurred."

The president would rather have this conversation be about nearly anything else in the world than slaves, slave trading, slavery, or blacks. The whole subject was a political liability. His base of supporters was a thinly held together coalition of Southerners and Northerners. They were unable, he estimated, to withstand a debate about slavery.

It was an issue he had hoped would go away. At least until after the election.

But it hadn't. The country was slowly creeping toward a confrontation on the issue. The Southern leaders would tolerate no consideration of the abolition, and suddenly the abolitionist movement had taken hold and was beginning to grow.

"Uh-huh." Van Buren cared about the future of America. Slavery was too complicated and too interwoven into the fabric of American life to think that it could be eradicated by simply being against it. What good would that do anyway?

"They killed everyone on board but two—two courageous men—who eventually managed to draw the attention of the American survey brig *Washington* to their plight," Calderon continued.

"Uh-huh." The president pulled strongly on his cigar. He held the smoke in a beat longer than usual. As if there were relief, somehow, in the sweet taste of the smoke.

"These slaves, imprisoned as we speak in New Haven, belong to Messrs. Montes and Ruiz. And, in the larger sense, to Spain. On behalf of Her Majesty, I must insist on their prompt return."

The president, put his cigar down and took a sip of his brandy. He expelled a heavy lungful of air. "Would you excuse us a moment?"

The minister seemed slightly uncomfortable but, in careful control, said, "Certainly." He stood up and stepped outside the door. The president wondered why this was on his desk already. Wasn't there someone charged with working out these kinds of problems?

"This is a Cuban vessel he's talking about?" he asked Hammond.

"Yes, sir."

"Cuban?" He wanted to be sure Hammond understood him. How many times would he have to repeat it before Hammond got the message? He didn't want to talk about it. He didn't want to have meetings about it. It was a Cuban ship.

"Yes, sir."

"Leder, I'm trying to drink my brandy after a very long day."

"I understand."

Hammond did understand. An explanation was in order. "I wasn't sure if this was something you personally wanted to address or leave to . . ."

And that was precisely what he had been waiting for. "There are what—three million Negroes in this country? Why on earth should I concern myself with these thirty-nine?" He picked up his cigar again. Stoked it, then took another draw. "I don't care how. Take care of it."

The president had sensed a definite danger in the news about the *Amistad*. But Lewis Tappan, a wealthy silk importer and, perhaps more important, a staunch and active abolitionist could see only the opportunity. This was a chance to make the lives of these Africans better and also to further the cause of the abolition of slavery.

The abolitionists, of which Lewis Tappan, as well as his brother Arthur, proudly counted himself a part, advocated the compulsory emancipation of African-American slaves. In 1839 they were a small but vocal group of Americans who found the institution of slavery abhorrent.

The American abolition movement had its roots in the evangelical movement of the 1820s. The American Anti-Slavery Society, for example, which was started in 1833, flooded the slave states with abolitionist literature and lobbied in Washington, D.C.

Lewis Tappan was a Puritan who had no tolerance for sin of any type. And he considered slavery to be a sin as damning as any other before the eyes of God. There was no compromise in him on these issues. Slavery had to be abolished for America to truly be a Christian society. He even strongly disagreed with the "free soilers," who were against the spread of slavery, but were unwilling to fight for its abolition. Tappan was a tall, substantial man whose convictions about slavery kept his energies focused on fund-raising and buttonholing influential people.

But at this particular moment, Tappan stood outside his warehouse as crates of goods and bolts of fabric were unloaded from a ship behind him. He was engaged in a discussion with five other men which had nothing to do with slavery whatsoever.

"Gentlemen, the key to all human interaction is what?" He paused for effect. "Isn't it trust? Why shouldn't the same be true of business transactions?"

Tappan peered into the faces of the men who were engrossed in his pitch. And it was indeed a pitch. He was determined to convince them that now was a perfect time to create a new business service. But as he talked, he noticed a well-dressed, obviously well-educated black man coming along the wharf with a newspaper tucked under his arm. Tappan made it a point to ignore the man and went on with his argument.

"That said, the service I'm suggesting would recommend just how much trust we can afford to offer."

The black man, Ted Joadson, moved deliberately and walked up to one of Tappan's white dockworkers. It was the man who was in charge of checking the accuracy of the supplies being off loaded. Joadson handed him the newspaper he'd been carrying. Only Tappan saw Joadson hand his shipping clerk the paper. He surmised it had something to do with the *Amistad*.

"This proposed service," one of the businessmen began, "this 'credit service' . . . how can it possibly guarantee that a man will honor his debt?"

Tappan could hear the sarcasm that was buried deep in the man's mind. "We would require him to sign his name, sir."

The man was stunned. "Sign his name?"

"That's right. To a piece of paper of some kind. He would thus be giving us his word of honor."

Tappan looked at them looking at him and knew they thought he was crazy. And perhaps he was. On all accounts. But his craziness had a purpose. He had not become as successful as he had by worrying about what people thought about his ideas. Right now he could clearly see they were not much impressed. And then he watched his shipping clerk walk away from Joadson and toward him. The clerk paused only an instant, long enough to hand the newspaper to Tappan.

Tappan didn't acknowledge even this exchange. Instead, he turned again to the businessman who was still talking.

"How would that guarantee anything?"

"Because we have faith, gentleman: in our fellow man and in the truism that honor, once got"—he unfolded the *New Haven Plain Dealer* paper just long enough to note its headline: MASSACRE AT SEA—"possesses a man for life."

A little later that morning, as the church clock struck eleven, Joadson walked side by side with Tappan as they crossed through the empty church and climbed a set of stairs in the back.

"The ship is called the *Amistad*," Joadson said. "Too small to be a transatlantic slaver." Theodore Joadson was one of the most distinguished-looking and sophisticated black men in New Haven. Everyone knew he volunteered his time and energy to the Anti-Slavery Society. He was considered an important member of the growing group of people, both publicly and privately, concerned with the plight of the Africans from the *Amistad*.

He was a good friend of Tappan's and assisted in the publication of the newspaper, though he held no formal position there. Joadson found himself moving between the black world and the one of white abolitionists. He considered it his duty to represent the feelings of black Americans in the fight against slavery.

Joadson presented an imposing picture of a black man who did not fear the power of white men. Indeed, he often carried himself as if he was unaware that others might treat him differently. In the manner of all the professional men of the time, he was almost never without his cane and cape. He was a free black American man and he wore his freedom large and unabashedly.

"They're plantation slaves then? West Indians . . . or . . ." Tappan paused as he realized that he was competing with the clanging of the chimes as they ascended the stairs and got closer to the workings of the church clock.

As they reached the top of the stairs, Joadson

stopped. "Not necessarily. They certainly don't look it. Not from the glimpse I caught of them on their way to jail. Several have these"—he drew lines on his cheeks with his fingers—"scars."

They were now up into the steeple of the church, in a room behind the clock. In this room amidst the exposed mechanism of the clock, revolving brass gears the size of plates, was a "newsroom" of sorts. This was where one of the country's leading abolitionist papers was published—by Tappan and edited by Joadson. Joadson and Tappan walked across the room. Several people, most of them black, were busy running the letterpress machine. The chimes of the clock were so loud that no words could be exchanged.

Finally Tappan made it to his desk, which was an old, scarred, wooden hulk that was cluttered with papers, books, and folders. When the chimes finally stopped, Joadson started right in.

"The arraignment's the day after tomorrow. I can only assume the charges will be murder."

Tappan nodded and picked up the newspaper again. He kept staring at the article about the massacre. Massacre. "Yes, well, I'll see what I can do about that. Perhaps a writ for illegal arrest and detainment to stall things." He paused. He watched as one of the men who ran the press handed a paper just off the press to Joadson.

Joadson looked at it quickly and passed it to

Tappan. The headline of their newspaper read FREEDOM FIGHT AT SEA. Tappan resumed his thought. "At the very least we can make sure they have good counsel."

7
Making Claims

On the day of the arraignment, the Africans were assembled and counted by guards in the courtyard. They were then methodically chained together and led out of the stockade and once again marched into the streets of New Haven.

Once out in the open, in the sunlight, the spirits of the prisoners lightened after the night in jail. As they were led toward the courthouse, one of the Africans called out in Mende to an elderly and quite elegantly dressed black coachman as he sat atop his carriage, *"Marda! Marda!"*

Buakei couldn't help but admonish him. "He's not a chief."

"Mori! Maha!"

"He's not a chief's adviser either."

"Ndeha! Nadiama!"

"And, he is not your brother."

"What is he then?"

83

And then Cinque, hearing this conversation, decided to add his opinion. "He's one of them."

"What do you mean, 'one of them'?"

"I mean," said Cinque, "He's not one of us." They all turned and looked at the stoic coachman as they passed.

From his vantage point, they represented a most curious sight. He imagined how afraid they must be, how disoriented. Looking at them made him think of his own parents, now long dead. This was how Africa came to America. In chains and against their will. Incapable of speaking the language. Incapable of walking the streets without wondering whether they have a right to do it.

They were led into the already crowded courtroom and jammed into a space set aside for them. There they sat in a wondrous daze. There were so many people. There was so much going on all at once. And they really had no idea what was happening. They knew what they had done. They knew that these people would probably try to enact some punishment on them.

"Hear-ye, hear-ye. For the State, the Commonwealth of Connecticut, in the capital of Hartford—New Haven . . . and of the District Court of the United States of America, in the year of our Lord, 1839. His Honorable Andrew T. Judson presiding. All rise."

As Judge Judson entered the courtroom and

proceeded to the bench, everyone except the Africans stood. The judge stared at them as if he had expected as much. He then looked up and out over the courtroom. He had a feeling this was bound to be a circus if he didn't exert a tight control over the proceedings. Judge Andrew T. Judson was a Connecticut Democrat, who was known not to support the abolitionist movement. In fact, before being appointed to the bench, he had prosecuted Prudence Crandal for attempting to open a school to teach black girls.

Judson looked at the prosecutor who was already rising to speak.

"Your Honor, if it pleases the court—"

"The Bench recognizes Federal Prosecutor Holabird."

William S. Holabird was the district attorney in Connecticut. He had not had time to get a full briefing on the government's position, but assumed his job would be to press for trial. "I wish to present to the court, Your Honor, the charges of piracy and murder against . . ." He wanted to look at the accused directly, so he turned in their direction. Holabird relished this opportunity to punish the slave mutineers.

At this moment, Lewis Tappan rose from a bench in the gallery, waving a handful of papers. "Your Honor, I have a petition for a writ of *habeas corpus* which I wish to present the court on behalf of the prisoners."

But Holabird, who had not anticipated any challenge quickly recovered. "Your Honor, I was speaking—"

Tappan asserted himself. "Yes I know, Mr. Holabird. You were reading charges which, whatever they might be, shall be rendered moot by this writ." Again he held the petition in the air.

"That petition for a writ, Mr. Tappan"— Holabird was warming to the challenge—"if indeed that's what it is, is moot. Unless and until an actual writ by some higher court, by some miracle, is granted."

The judge spoke into the charged air. "Mr. Holabird is correct, Mr. Tappan."

Holabird turned to Tappan. "And if you would, sir, while I know it is your custom, please kindly refrain from impersonating the lawyer you so clearly are not." And, with that, Holabird figured he had mortally wounded Tappan and was free to proceed. So he turned now to face the judge.

"As I was saying—" But Holabird was interrupted again, this time by policemen pushing through the crowd by the door. Into the path they made, stepped a tall, self-assured American who just happened to be the United States Secretary of State, John Forsyth. And with him was Angel Calderon, the Spanish ambassador.

Judge Judson could see clearly now that this was going to be a difficult trial. He had thirty-nine blacks in his courtroom. He wasn't sure whether they were pirates or slaves or what. He didn't know whose they were if they were slaves. And now he had presidential cabinet members and foreign dignitaries pushing their way into his court. It was just a little overwhelming already.

John Forsyth didn't hesitate and didn't stop moving through the courtroom until he was before the judge. "Your Honor."

"Mr. Secretary." Judson found his throat a little dry.

"I'm here on behalf of the President of the United States, representing the claims of Her Majesty, Queen Isabella of Spain, as concerns our mutual Treaty on the High Seas of 1795." Forsyth carried himself with the utmost confidence. He had been charged by Van Buren to expeditiously dispose of the *Amistad* affair by reminding the court that the Treaty of 1795 with Spain, which provided for any captured property on the high seas to be returned to its proper country.

Forsyth believed in states' rights and felt that the Federal government should not interfere with slavery. He considered the institution to be one that was under the control of each individual state. The truth was that Forsyth himself was the owner of a few household slaves and honestly believed they were a necessity.

In the gallery, Joadson and Tappan exchanged looks, each wondering where the case was going

and why so many powerful people were interested in it. If John Forsyth was involved, it meant
that the president was involved. It was the first
indication that the concept of "checks and bal-
ances" might be challenged in this case.

At this moment Roger Baldwin quietly glided
into the court. He wasn't sure what had led him
to the courtroom. He himself was a young attorney with a robust practice, although his clients
were almost exclusively common folk. Not the
kind that paid well. But in a way he'd felt com-
pelled to be there. And the more he thought
about the situation, the more interested he was
as to his value to those who were defending the
Africans.

The judge softened his voice and said to the
secretary, "You have my attention, sir."

"These slaves, Your Honor," District Attorney
Holabird began, "are by rights the property of
Spain and as such, under Article 9 of said treaty,
are to be returned posthaste. Said treaty taking
precedence over all other claims and jurisdic-
tions."

And just as the courtroom had seemed to settle
down, Lieutenant Gedney interrupted the proceedings by shouting, "Them slaves belong to me
and my mate, Your Majesty!" It had been the two
lieutenants who had captured the *Amistad* and
they were in court now to claim them as salvage.
It was often common practice to allow the cap-

tains who captured pirate ships to keep some or all of their cargo, perhaps even the ships, as salvage.

The judge looked at them, even more stunned. This trial had not even begun and it was already testing his abilities. "And who be you two gentlemen?"

Gedney produced a document from his coat and began to read. "We, Thomas R. Gedney and Richard W. Meade, whilst commissioned U.S. Naval officers, stand before this court as private citizens and do hereby claim salvage on the high seas of the Spanish ship *Amistad* and all her cargo."

He then handed the paper to the judge. "Here you go, sir."

Judge Judson took a look at the document. How ridiculous was this going to get? He looked out over his courtroom again. He stared this time at Cinque, who sat there in apparent bewilderment. Judson wondered what he and his countrymen were thinking.

Secretary Forsyth tried to stifle a laugh. "Your Honor."

Judge Judson ignored the politician and spoke to Lieutenant Meade. "You wish to make this claim over that of the Queen of Spain?"

"Well, where was she, pray, when we was fightin' the winds to bring this vessel in?" A giggle rippled through the courtroom.

At that, Angel Calderon spoke up. "Her Majesty, the Queen of Spain was ruling a country! Your Honor, these officers' claims are . . . are . . ." The Spaniard seemed frozen in midsentence, unable to find the right word in English that would fit.

But Secretary Forsyth was not so hampered. "Absurd. Inane."

"Insane?" Lieutenant Meade intended to intimidate both the secretary and the Spanish ambassador.

But Forsyth shot back at him, "In-*ane*. Look it up."

To complicate matters even further, Lieutenant Gedney joined the argument. "And who might you be, sir?"

"Secretary of State of the United States of America . . . sir."

Judge Judson had heard enough. He slammed down his gavel. "Gentlemen, clearly this matter will require a day or two of review. The court will then reconvene and respond to each of the claims presented here today." He took a breath and heard no sound except that which came from his body. He then looked at Lieutenants Meade and Gedney. "Even yours."

He leaned forward, addressing everyone. "Now, I'm going to take it on faith there is no one else present I need to hear from." But he was thwarted once again as another voice broke from the silence of the gallery.

"Your Honor. Here are the true owners of these slaves."

And then in came José Ruiz and Pedro Montes, escorted by yet another lawyer, who was addressing the bench even as they approached. "On their behalf, and in possession of a Receipt-for-Purchase executed in Havana, Cuba, June 26, 1839, I do hereby call upon this court to immediately surrender these goods." He gestured at the Africans. "And that ship out there. To my clients, José Ruiz and Pedro Montes."

Judge Judson quickly tried to regain the reins of this runaway carriage. He duly noted the petition by Ruiz and Montes and adjourned for the day. The Africans were escorted from the courtroom, having no more information than they did before. Except that Cinque could tell by the number and variety of the apparent rivals that he and his fellow prisoners were indeed of considerable value.

Roger Baldwin had stood quietly in the back of the courtroom as the proceedings had unfolded. Now he sought to engage the men who seemed most connected to the prisoners. "Mr. Tappan." He advanced on Tappan and Joadson, who had left the courtroom and were now in the corridor. Baldwin virtually ingored Joadson. He held a card of introduction out to Tappan. "How do you do? My name is Roger Baldwin. Attorney-at-law."

Tappan took the card and looked at it. He took a quick survey of the man. The scuffed shoes and cheap gray suit didn't make for a strong statement. For a moment, there was an awkward air between the three men. Baldwin briefly glanced at Joadson, but turned quickly away. He was unsure how to address a black man who seemed more white in his ways than many white men he knew.

"You're a real estate attorney?" Tappan asked wondering why Baldwin was standing there taking up their time.

"Real estate, inventories, and other contestable assets, sir."

"Can I help you with something?" Tappan was anxious to move on.

"Well, I don't know." Baldwin had already estimated that Tappan would not be inclined to entertain a proposition such as the one he wanted to offer and felt that showing a little irreverence might prove to be to his advantage. "What do you do?"

Tappan looked at him as if he were mad. He was not accustomed to people not knowing him or how successful he was. "I own various businesses and banks, sir."

"Oh well, then. As a matter of fact, you probably could help me." Baldwin laughed at his own attempt at humor. Tappan was stone faced. "But that's not why I came over. I'd like to help you."

"Me?"

"Yes. You see, I get people's property back for them, Mr. Tappan. Or sometimes get it taken away." Baldwin now regarded Tappan. He couldn't read the man.

For his part, Tappan hadn't a clue as to what Baldwin was talking about. He nodded hesitantly.

"Clearly this is a property issue," Baldwin continued. "All of these claims, every one of them, speaks to the issue of ownership."

Tappan wasn't really listening carefully anymore. Baldwin had taken too long and perhaps the wrong tack in stating his purpose. "Thank you for your interest, Mr. . . . ?"

"Baldwin."

"Mr. Baldwin. But I'm afraid what's needed here is a criminal attorney. A trial lawyer."

"Uh-huh. Well, intending no disrespect, if that were the way to go, I wouldn't have bothered coming over here. Would I have?"

Tappan was a man of conscience. Of commitment. He was for the downtrodden and the abused. But impudence? He had no patience for impudence. He stared at Baldwin, who seemed oblivious and smiled back at him.

"I bid you gentlemen good afternoon." With that, Baldwin turned and took his leave. Tappan and Joadson watched him walk away. But suddenly he stopped and turned back. "Did I give you my card?"

Tappan looked at Joadson and then to Baldwin, holding up the card as proof. Baldwin nodded and walked away again.

8

On Display

"Wherever the moon eventually settles, becomes the village arena."

The machinations and intrigue associated with the trial of the former inhabitants of the *Amistad* meant little as yet to the Africans in a real way. They were alone. They were still in chains. Still held captive by white men who fought over them as if they were gold. Though they were fed better and were suddenly the subject of newspaper reports and commentaries, they were still wretched.

As night fell around them, the jail settled into a multifaceted community just as it had on each of the ships, especially the *Amistad*. Fala had slipped into the darkness held within. He had begun to separate himself more and more. He was trying to maintain contact with the part of him that could not be dominated. As he pondered, he dug through the dirt of the floor in front of him. He'd sift through the earth until he found a small stone, like the one he now lifted from the ground. He looked at it carefully, but decided its surface was not abrasive enough for the task for which he intended to use it.

In the next cell, Buakei stared out past the bars across the courtyard where Maseray and the children crouched in a corner. He couldn't help wondering what would be the thing which would make a difference in their futures. He thought about what had happened in court and couldn't help saying to Cinque, who shared his cell, "I don't think anything was decided, do you?"

Cinque heard him and wanted to say yet again, how frustrating it was not to be able to speak the language of these white people. But instead he said, "It took a lot of people to not decide anything."

Buakei nodded. That was so true. Throughout the jail, the Africans were busy occupying themselves. Some played a kind of dice game. Some traded stories. Occasionally there were eruptions of laughter or teasing.

Into this environment Colonel Pendleton invited New Haven aristocrats who, for a shilling, were curious to see the "animals in their natural habitat" as he put it.

"Be forewarned, what you are about to see is not for the faint of heart." He injected as much drama into the presentation as he could muster.

He couldn't help overhearing one of the women say to her date, "My heart is pounding."

"Ladies in particular, take care." He began playing on the woman's skittishness. "Be very careful not to stray too close to the bars. We're armed, but remember, so too was the crew of the *Amistad*. Just one shilling and you shall see what many white men fear."

Buakei saw them. The lanterns that lit their way, yet shrouded them in shadows making it hard to see clearly, but he saw them coming. "What's this? Another council? So late at night?"

One of the Temne, Biah, looked at him like he was crazy. "Don't be stupid, Mende, look at them. Look how they're dressed."

As the party drew closer, Buakei could see better. He could see the hats that were like little tree stumps stuck on the heads of the white people, who were buttoned tight with fancy cloth from neck to toe. And the women seemed unnaturally endowed with lace and metal forms which increased their silhouettes, but not them.

"They're entertainers," Biah said with a slight air of impatience.

Buakei watched them now in a different way. He expected them to break into song or dance or something. But they didn't. Instead they stared back at him in nearly the same curious way he was looking at them. Suddenly, throughout the jail, there was silence as everyone stopped what they were doing and watched the visitors.

Buakei whispered to Biah, "I don't see any instruments."

Biah agreed with a reluctant nod. The two groups stared at each other, waiting for someone to do something. And someone did. Fala had found a stone that fit his needs. Everyone heard him at the same time. It was a soft, grinding sound, like a knife being sharpened. And everyone looked in Fala's direction to find him sitting there, with the strangest expression on his face as he used the rock to sharpen his teeth. And no one knew exactly what to say.

In Washington, the Africans were causing a different kind of disturbance as it seemed they were destined to do in all facets of American life. These thirty-nine adults and four children were having a profound effect in a myriad of ways. But it had not quite reached John Quincy Adams, who sat in Congress, as South Carolina's Democratic Representative Henry Laurens Pinckney spoke to a sparsely filled House of Representatives.

"In closing, I call upon our distinguished colleague from Massachusetts, Representative John Quincy Adams, to reweigh his unmet and unprecedented attempt to convert this eccentric bequest of—let's be frank, a bunch of junk—of one James Smithson into a so-called 'Institute of National Treasure.' "

Not many among those still in attendance had

the slightest notion of what Representative Henry
Pinckney was talking about. But at the mention of
the former president, John Quincy Adams, now
seventy-two and a congressman, everyone turned
in his direction. What they saw was a white-
haired old man who sat fully relaxed and deep in
his seat, eyes closed and apparently in the midst
of a catnap. There were a few titters and giggles
from the floor.

"Perhaps Mr. Adams is meditating on his response." Pinckney sought this opportunity to attempt to reduce the elder statesman's influence.
And it was working. People began to laugh out
loud. Loud enough to awake the average sleeping
man. But Adams was not the average sleeping
congressman. He seemed beyond the realm of
consciousness.

And then he yawned and stretched ever so
slightly. "Had I thought your remarks worthy of
any kind of riposte, Representative Pinckney, be
assured you would have heard from me *hours*
ago." And with that he closed his eyes again.

A little later Adams and his secretary, Mr.
Wright, were slowly walking down the foyer
staircase of the Congressional Building.

"He says, Mr. President, that he *must* see you."

"Who is this, you say?"

"Mr. Tappan. Lewis Tappan."

Adams stopped and said. "I *must* see him? I am *required* to see him?"

"No. Of course not, sir. He *requests* an audience." Wright sensed Adams was looking for a middle course.

"I see. He requests. Yes. Do I know this Mr. . . . ?"

"Tappan. Yes, sir, you do. You've met him on, ah . . . countless occasions."

"Yes. Of course. Tappan. Well, man, see to it." Adams turned into his office.

Wright sighed heavily and followed him in. "Yes, sir."

Two days later, Tappan and Joadson stood in Adams's office. Tappan and Adams shook hands, though Adams truly didn't remember him.

"Lewis. So nice to see you again." Adams did remember that he was *supposed* to know him.

"And you, sir." Tappan stepped back and gestured to Joadson. "And this is Theodore Joadson."

Adams nodded to the black man and said a quick, "How do you do."

Joadson, however had been looking forward with great excitement to meeting the former president. "It's a great honor to meet you, sir."

Adams looked around, searching for some way out of the awkwardness he felt. What was he doing with these two? What was this all about?

And then he had an idea, an instinct really. He'd caught a glimpse of color in some corner of his mind and on an impulse said, "Shall we stroll in the gardens?"

The Congressional Gardens were one of Adams's favorite places to go. He loved the variety of flora there. Indeed, he was more preoccupied with the plants and flowers than with what Tappan, who had begun making his plea, was saying.

"I believe this case has great significance. Our Secretary of State has already deemed it worthy of his attention, supporting the Queen of Spain in her claims that the Africans belong to her. Then there are others making claims. Among them . . ."

Joadson watched the spectacle. Tappan talked. Adams seemed to care about everything but what was being said.

"What season is it?" Adams spoke into empty space. The other two men were stunned and didn't quite know what to say. But he continued. "Without consulting a calendar, there are two ways of knowing for certain."

He then pointed to a group of trees along the perimeter of the garden. "The leaves on the maple trees are almost gone, and the fact that the president isn't home on Pennsylvania Avenue." He chuckled at his own joke, though neither Joadson nor Tappan were swift enough to catch its full power. They both held weak smiles.

"Do you really think Van Buren cares about the whims of a nine-year-old girl wearing a tiara? I can assure, having been there, only one thing occupies his thoughts at this time of the year: being all things to all people. Which of course means being nothing to no one. In other words, getting himself reelected." With that he kneeled to examine the brilliant color of a rose.

Tappan and Joadson again threw glances between them. Tappan was ready to cast caution to the wind. "Will you help us?" The old man seemed not to hear. "Mr. Adams?"

"What?"

"As an advocate for the abolition of slavery, will you help us?"

"I'm neither friend nor foe to the abolitionist cause. No, I won't help you." He then set about carefully taking a cutting from the plant.

Tappan was about to respond when Joadson interrupted. "Sir. I know you. I know as much about you and your presidency as any man. And your father's."

At the mention of his father, Adams's face twitched with a slight smile. He thought about his father and how much he missed him. How much he'd learned and how happy he'd been that his father had lived to see him also ascend to the White House.

"You were a child at his side when he helped invent America. You in turn have devoted your life to refining that noble invention. But there remains one task still left undone." Here Joadson tried to calm himself. This was all passion and fire for him. Working toward the end of slavery was what had kept him going. All of his research and writing, all of his intellectual energy were being applied to this goal. "One vital task the founding fathers left to their sons before their thirteen colonies could precisely be called United States. Crushing slavery."

Tappan was just a little put off by Joadson's fervor and the fact that he, a black man would dare to lecture a white man, particularly a former U.S. president in such a manner. But he decided not to say anything.

At any rate, Joadson had no intention of stopping. "Your record confirms you're an abolitionist, President Adams, even if you won't. Whether you want to admit it or not. You belong with us."

Adams was quite impressed by the black man's speech. He slowly turned and took a good long look at the man. Tappan fidgeted uncomfortably.

"You're quite the scholar, Mr. Joadson, aren't you? Quite the . . . historian. Let me tell you something about that 'quality' if I might. Without an accompanying mastery of at least one tenth's its measure of grace, such erudition is worthless." He paused and considered his own words. Then he stood and prepared to leave. "Take it from one who knows Now, if you gentlemen will excuse me."

But Tappan was unwilling to let him go. He elbowed Joadson aside with uncharacteristic rudeness. He had one last card to play. Outright flattery. "We know we aimed high coming to see you, sir, but . . ."

"Well, aim lower. Find yourselves someone who, ah . . . whose inspiration blossoms the more you lose." He looked at the cutting he held in his hand, pulled it closer to his body, turned, and walked away down the garden path.

9
What Are "They"?

Roger Baldwin's law practice didn't suffer from lack of clients. Perhaps their lack of ability to pay him in cash was sometimes a problem. But he did not want for clients. He had become rather specialized in the litigation of matters regarding ownership and property and he wasn't very discriminating in his clientele. He often took cases in which he was paid in all manner of ways.

For example, as Joadson and Tappan squeezed their way into his crowded waiting area, they saw the young attorney emerge from his inner office, carrying his appointment book, escorting a man, obviously a farmer, for he carried the reins to two goats that followed them out of the office. There was also a rather large woman who sat there nursing a baby. Sitting next to her, trying not to look at the woman's considerable teat, sat a man, a seaman, who had a hunk of crudely carved ivory fashioned into a fist and placed where his hand should have been. And in front of them paced a man of behemoth proportions who looked as if he had walked out of the mountains.

Baldwin was in midsentence. "I don't care about the fence. Tear it down."

"He'll just put up another." The man spoke back with resignation.

"And you'll tear *it* down. And the one after that. Until he produces a record of survey that says otherwise, you are completely within your rights."

"Tear it down . . ." The man seemed incredulous and then nodded his agreement. Baldwin firmly patted his back and ushered him to the door. The hooves of the goats clacking on the wooden floor behind them.

Baldwin saw Tappan and Joadson, but ignored them. Instead, he flipped open his appointment book. "Mr. Gutwillig." The man with the artificial hand followed Baldwin into his office.

Joadson looked at Tappan and smiled. They deserved that. After all, it had been Baldwin who had first come to them. And they had dismissed him as a gadfly and a meddler. Now, they found themselves in his office, hoping he'd take the time to see them again.

Roger Baldwin had graduated from Yale College with honors, and after studying law, had been admitted to the bar in 1814. He was known to have a special interest in the cases that involved people who were incapable of providing for their own defense.

Eventually Baldwin did finish with his clients. He finally walked out of his office, rolling down his sleeves. He didn't seem surprised at all that Joadson, who stood by the door, and Tappan, who was thumbing through the day's paper, had waited. "Come gentlemen, let's take a walk, shall we?"

Baldwin walked with a brisk gait. Joadson, though silent, liked the brash lawyer. Tappan was almost huffing trying to keep up. Finally they reached the wharf, where Baldwin slowed to a stroll.

"These old Dutch land grants are driving everyone mad. I'm working on a case now—you'll find this as interesting as I do"—Joadson wondered if he meant him, too—"involving a Peekskill grant from 1680, deeding four thousand acres to the youngest heir. A son. And in perpetuity. Specifically forbidding transfer of the land through his sisters."

Baldwin was totally lost in what seemed like an esoteric consideration. "Ah, but what's coming to light now is that the son had carnal relations with his mother. Thus his sister is in fact his daughter and the rightful legal heir after all." He smiled and shrugged. "You know how cold and lonely those upstate winters can be. . . ." He abruptly stopped talking. And then he switched his attention completely.

There was an old man slowly approaching them. Baldwin knew him to be Bomoseen, an Abnaki Indian. Bomoseen was bent over as if he had been carrying a great weight for a long time. A heavy fish net on his back was full of live crabs.

"Bomoseen," Baldwin said brightly.

The man moved his mouth, but neither of the three men heard what he said.

"You're looking well."

Joadson eyed Baldwin and wondered about the relationship between the crab catcher and the lawyer.

Baldwin kept right on talking, even though Bomoseen had already passed them by. "That's right. Good day to you." And then to Tappan and Joadson, he said, "I can never understand a word he says."

Tappan looked at Joadson in a kind of bewilderment. He decided to ignore the entire exchange with the Abnaki and go back to Baldwin's remark about the case he was working on. "So that's the sort of case you've been dealing with lately? Uh . . . land grants?"

"Just one of many. Business is brisk." He stopped outside the Harbor Tavern and went inside. Again Joadson and Tappan followed. Inside, they were immediately enveloped by the smell of ale and old wood. It was dark and in contrast with the hot sun outside, cool. It was a busy time of the day and the tavern was quite crowded and noisy. It was peopled mostly by men of the sea and other people, both men and women who made money from the flow of ships in and out of the harbor.

Baldwin directed them to a table in the corner as they walked amongst cold-eyed stares and threatening gestures. There was laughter in one area; a budding argument in another. People waiting, it seemed, for something to happen. For their ship to come in or to put out.

After the men were seated, Baldwin ordered fish and potatoes. For the longest time they were all silent, acclimating themselves. When the food came, Baldwin attacked his with great gusto.

Meanwhile, Joadson could barely contain himself. This was serious business. This case was quickly and very obviously becoming of critical importance in the fight to end slavery. If they couldn't find an adequate defense for Cinque and his people, the opportunity might slip away. He looked at Baldwin, who ate heartily. "If the courts award them to Spain, they'll be sent to Cuba and executed. If those two lieutenants prevail, they'll most likely sell them back to Spain, and they'll be executed." He paused; he wasn't sure Baldwin was actually listening. "If Ruiz and Montes are successful in their claims—"

Baldwin abruptly looked up from his plate.

"I'm a little confused by something. What are they worth to you? How's the sea bass, Mr. Tappan?"

Tappan stopped eating. Joadson stopped talking. Each man tried in his own way to maintain a level of dignified control. "What do you mean by that remark?" Tappan took his turn.

"I can see the concern on your face. You needn't be concerned. The fish is fresh here. It's your favorite places uptown you should worry about. By the time it gets up there, it's been on the cart for two days."

Tappan let his eyes blink twice before he said with restrained exasperation, "I meant your other remark."

"Ah . . . you're concerned about what this is going to cost."

Now he had ripped it. "In point of fact, sir, it was the furthest thing from my mind. We're discussing the case, not its expense."

"The case. Yes. Of course. The case is much simpler than you think, Mr. Tappan. It's like . . . ah . . . anything . . . isn't it? Land, livestock, heirlooms . . . what have you. Determine who the rightful owner is and victory draws within spitting distance."

But Tappan couldn't help focusing on the way Baldwin considered the issues that were present. "Livestock?" He looked again at Joadson.

But either Baldwin didn't hear him, or didn't

care. "Consider, the only way one may legally sell or purchase slaves is if they are born slaves. As on a plantation. I'm right, aren't I?"

"Yes," Joadson agreed.

"So are they?"

"Are they . . . what?" Tappan asked, because it was exactly what he was thinking.

"Yes." Baldwin nodded now, as a man who had sprung a trap on a beloved foe or turned his hole card over in a friendly game of poker.

Joadson smiled. "We don't know for sure, but we very much doubt it." It was a very interesting point. One both he and Tappan had overlooked. Who said these people were slaves? Did just being black in a white man's world make a person a slave? Could their society really mean that? With all the talk of equality and freedom? With all the promises America had made to its inhabitants? Would being black be forever a sentence to domination? Could this be God's plan for white men? To be the masters of black men? He thought not.

"Let's say they are. If they are, then they are possessions, and no more deserving of a criminal trial than a bookcase or plow. And we can all go home," Baldwin said.

Joadson was lost in the consideration of himself as someone else's thing, someone else's possession. Tappan reared back to respond, but Baldwin didn't give him the chance.

"Let's say on the other hand, they aren't slaves. If they aren't, then they were illegally acquired, weren't they? Forget mutiny. Forget piracy and murder and all the rest." By this point both Joadson and Tappan were with him, leaning forward, caught up in his passion. The pure clarity of truth and logic. This was no impassioned plea for the souls of the Africans. "Those are subsequent . . . irrelevant occurrences. Ignore everything but the preeminent issue at hand. The wrongful transfer of stolen goods." He shrugged to underscore the simplicity of his argument. "Either way, we win."

Tappan had missed the "truth" or more precisely, had found Baldwin's truth to be reprehensible. How dare he talk about people as if they weren't human beings? "Sir, this war must be waged on the battlefield of righteousness."

"The what?" Baldwin fought a smile.

"It would be against everything I stand for to let this deteriorate into an exercise in the vagaries of legal minutiae."

Now Baldwin stared at him. "I don't know what you're talking about. I'm talking about the heart of the matter."

"As am I. It's our destiny as, as abolitionists and Christians to save these people."

Baldwin sat back in his chair.

"These are people, Mr. Baldwin. Not livestock. Did Christ hire a lawyer to get him off on technicalities? He went to the cross, sir. Nobly. And you know why? To make a statement. As must we."

Baldwin considered Tappan's words. He knew why the man talked so fervently and why this was such an important point for him to make. "But Christ lost," he said flatly. They were all silent again. And then he thought he'd try a different tack. "You, I think—or at least you, Mr. Joadson, want to win, don't you? I certainly do. I sometimes don't get *paid* unless I do."

Joadson had listened to both men speak. He understood Tappan and agreed with him. He himself was a man of faith and was often identified with the religious leadership among some of his people. But there was also something powerful in Baldwin's argument that Joadson thought they shouldn't dismiss: the idea of winning. Using the most expedient and effective way to win. That was what Baldwin represented. It was time they had someone like him on their side.

Baldwin kept talking. "Which brings us back to the earlier question. Of worth. In order to do a better job than the attorney who represented the Son of God, I'll require two and a half dollars a day."

Joadson smiled and nodded to Tappan. He was sold. It was too reasonable an offer, with too confident a lawyer not to take him up on it. Tappan on the other hand was willing to go along, but he retained deep reservations about Baldwin. Christ had not "lost" anything. How dare he make such analogy? In his death, Christ won. But in this fight, he'd use Baldwin because it was clear that the forces arrayed against the Africans were significant and extended across even the Atlantic Ocean.

They finished their meals and paid the bill. Baldwin didn't even consider making a contribution.

"He may be right, Mr. Tappan," Joadson said as Baldwin strolled away from them down the wharf, blending in with the dockworkers.

"You're saying that only because he's the last person on the list."

"Maybe so."

It had been a long time since Colonel Stanton Pendleton's jail had been so full. But he liked the attention and the responsibility. And he liked it that his wife now had something to occupy her time. Even though he knew that she was a little uncomfortable that he had brought three young African girls into the house.

As they sat down to breakfast that morning, the maid, a black woman and legally free, placed a bowl of porridge in front of each of the three skimpily dressed girls. Then she served the colonel and his wife.

As the maid left, the girls began to eat, their fingers dipping into the thick white cereal. Pendleton watched them, slightly amused. His wife, as if she shared the table with royalty, daintily and most delicately used her spoon. Each of the girls looked up and watched the fat white woman eat.

Mrs. Pendleton smiled at them. She knew she had their attention. It wouldn't take long before they would be as well mannered as any group of colored girls could be.

Outside, in the prison courtyard, the prisoners had reverted again to the same tribal encampments that divided the *Amistad*. On the ship there had been an unnatural eeriness to the small enclaves. But on the ground, within the walls of the prison, with steaming pots of rice as the "village" center, it seemed more normal. There were the Mende, Temne, Fula, Sherbro, Kono, and Lokkos. Of course, the lone Kissi, Fala, as always kept off to himself, but usually stayed in the Temne territory.

Cinque and Buakei were standing near a barred opening in the thick stone wall of the prison. They watched the neighborhood residents file into the chapel across the street. But standing to the side of the church, looking directly at the two Africans, were three missionaries.

"Who are they, do you think?" Buakei said without looking at Cinque.

"I don't know. But they look miserable," he

said as he noted their somber demeanor, and most certainly the black robes.

Buakei watched the three drop to their knees. "What's this? What are they doing now?"

Cinque watched the missionaries pray. He didn't know or care that much what they were doing. "Looks like they're getting sick," was all he said as he glanced away from them and back into the courtyard. He found Fala sitting alone. No friends. No food. Cinque picked up a bowl of rice from the Mende pot and carried it across the courtyard and held it out to the small, but menacing Fala.

Fala looked at him, took the food, and sat it on the ground. Then, as Cinque watched, the Kissi fumbled in a little pouch and extracted a bracelet. Cinque held his hand up to say that it wasn't necessary, but Fala would not be denied and pressed the bracelet into his hand. Cinque took it and as he inspected it, Fala began eating.

Cinque looked up and could see that Yamba across the courtyard looked at him disparagingly. The Temne tolerated but didn't really like Fala. Cinque wasn't completely sure why, but he realized no one ever really spent time talking to Fala.

"I've been wanting to ask you," he began, not knowing if what he was about to say was a good idea or not. "Why do you sharpen your teeth like sticks?"

Fala considered his question and then motioned for Cinque to move closer to him. Which Cinque did. And then Fala whispered, "For the ladies."

Cinque smiled, as did Fala. But then Fala suddenly began coughing, and when he pulled his hand away from his mouth, Cinque saw that he had coughed blood. "How long has this been going on? You're sick," he said to the Kissi.

Fala quickly turned and walked away from Cinque, who just stood there watching him, wondering what he could do.

10
The Power of Place

"Running begins in small steps."

Everyone in the prison stopped what they were doing when the gate opened and two guards entered carrying a small wooden table and two chairs. They set the table and chairs down in the center of the courtyard. Behind them walked three men. Two were Joadson and Baldwin. The third man was Professor Josiah Gibbs, a Harvard linguist who had been enlisted to help them communicate with the Africans. Baldwin and Gibbs sat, Joadson remained standing.

Baldwin looked around him and saw the various fires burning. He could feel everyone's eyes on them. He thought he might break the ice by approaching one of the prisoners near him. "How do you do?" he said rising and extending his hand.

The man Baldwin addressed was Kinnah, of the Sherbro tribe. The man got up from his crouched position and walked over. Baldwin offered his hand. But Kinnah simply stared at it. He then picked up the table and unceremoniously moved it to the other side of his tribe's unmarked, but well-known territory. When he went to pick the table up, Gibbs and Baldwin almost jumped back. They weren't sure, at first, what was going on. After he set the table down, he walked back to Baldwin and drew a short line in the dirt with his foot. Two others from his tribe then moved the chairs.

But that was not the end of it. The Sherbros had clearly moved the table and chairs into Konoland. The Konos were quickly up and moving the furniture outside of their territorial boundaries.

Joadson now broke a smile. He understood the significance of tribe although it was an intellectual understanding. He could see on the faces of his African brothers an emotional and a spiritual connection to whatever land they had claimed for themselves. Baldwin and Gibbs were struck dumb and just watched as the table and chairs continued their journey across the courtyard.

The Konos dropped the furniture in the Mende area. They moved it to the land of the Temne, who finally moved it right up against the stone wall in a corner of the prison's courtyard.

Joadson couldn't stop smiling as he, Baldwin, and Gibbs made their way to the new location of their "office." As they reached the table, Baldwin took a stack of papers out of his bag. He motioned to Gibbs to sit down again.

But Yamba had quietly walked up to them. He studied Joadson. "You're big . . . but not that big." He spoke in Temne so Joadson had no idea of what he was saying.

"I'm sorry. I don't understand." He looked into Yamba's eyes. He suddenly felt a deep sense of connection to these people. The fact that communicating with them was going to be difficult wasn't important. They were black like himself; they came from the same land of his ancestors.

And of course, Yamba could not understand him. They stared at each other until Baldwin broke their connection. "Excuse me," he said, "how do you do? My name is Roger Baldwin. This is Theodore Joadson of the Anti-Slavery Society. And Professor Gibbs, a . . . ah . . . linguist."

Another African, Gola, had walked up behind Yamba and asked, "What does he want?"

"What do you want?" Yamba asked Baldwin, who looked to the professor for a translation.

But Gibbs could only shrug at his confusion. "Keep talking. Get them to talk," he said as he began making notes in his book.

Across the courtyard, Cinque, Fala and Buakei watched Yamba and the visitors. They couldn't hear what was being said but they watched the gestures of the group to make their interpretations.

Buakei leaned closer to Cinque. "What do you think? Is he here to help us?"

"I don't know. He reminds me of that Fula back home who hires himself out to scrape elephant dung from the crop rows."

"A dung scraper might be just the kind of man we need right now," Buakei said, as he walked away.

"Have you seen this before?" Baldwin unsheathed the sword they had confiscated from the *Amistad*. It was Cinque's, the one he had used to kill Ferrer and the other sailor. Yamba recognized it immediately.

"I could kill you with my hands before you raise that sword shoulder high," he said just to let them know he wasn't afraid. If Baldwin and Gibbs had understood him, they would have quickly made their exit. But this conversation was as surreal as the entire adventure. No one understood anything that the other was saying.

The professor shrugged his shoulders again in exasperation. Baldwin stared at the saber a moment and then handed it to a guard. He then picked up a rolled-up map and put it on the table.

"Where are you from?" he asked.

Kinnah, who was still there with Yamba, asked, "What did he say?"

"I didn't understand a word of it. It's gibber-ish," Yamba answered.

Gibbs, who'd been listening carefully, said to Baldwin, "He said, I think, 'show me the map.' "

"Who is this little man that looks and talks like a bird?" Kinnah asked Yamba.

Baldwin quickly unrolled the map and beck-oned Yamba to come closer. But Yamba did not move. Baldwin pointed to the continent of Africa. "Is this where you're from? Africa?"

Kinnah was again right in Yamba's ear. "What does he want?"

"He's an idiot," Yamba responded. "He just likes to hear himself talk."

"Baldwin then pointed to the Caribbean Ocean on the map. "Or is this where you were born?" he said in weak Spanish. "Were you born in the West Indies?"

Yamba turned to face his countryman. "All three of them are idiots."

Baldwin asked Gibbs, "What did he say?"

Complete flustered, Gibbs let out a heavy sigh. "I think he said 'we have to go now.' "

Finally after more than an hour of trying to communicate, the visitors left the prison. In the carriage, as they rode away, Joadson was mildly discouraged, but found his contact with the pris-oners invigorating. They were so strong. Not compliant or malleable. They were thoroughly

African. Baldwin, on the other hand, was quite despondent.

"They're hopeless. You're hopeless, Professor, to be honest." He considered his legal position. Even without being able to communicate, he still felt he had a good case. "I don't need anything from them anyway."

Gibbs was a little put off by the young, arrogant Baldwin's attitude. "I think, sir, it's West African. But you have to understand that there are over twenty languages and a hundred dialects spoken there."

"Well, it's not Spanish, that much I can tell you," Baldwin nearly spat back.

11

Slave Owners

Slave Owners

At nine years old, Queen Isabella II of Spain often had a great deal of time to ruminate about the type of country she wished to govern. Time, yes, but capacity was another matter. There would be so much yet for her to learn. For now, she had interests to be sure. Curiosities. America was one such curiosity.

General Espartero, her regent, had put a letter in front of her and taken a step back, awaiting her signature. She read the letter aloud. She liked that—the sound of her voice.

"As you may perceive, I wish you to act promptly before this matter of the Africans becomes a weight on our two countries."

The general cleared his throat. "Great countries, Your Majesty."

She nodded. "Our *great* countries. After all, the business of great countries is to do business. Slavery is our pillar of commerce in the New World.

Without it, our good will and excellent trade relations should be imperiled. Without it, we might have been denied the glory of aiding you in your virtuous rebellion against the British."

Isabella looked up from her letter to see the general smiling at her. She adjusted her tiara and continued. "As slave-owning nations we must together stand firm. Speak the words of humanness for the masses of your citizens, but hold tightly to the power that protects them. That power of course, is their wealth. The Africans must never go free. With sincerest admiration, Isabella II, Queen of all Spain." As she finished, she felt completely satisfied.

She signed it and sent it on its way with the good general.

It eventually found its way to President Van Buren while he was on the campaign trail. He was on the presidential train when Secretary Forsyth handed him the letter. He read it and finally, after glancing at the signature twice, stared blankly up at Hammond and Forsyth.

"I thought you took care of this . . . annoying business," he said to Forsyth.

"We are, ah, in the process of, ah, taking care of it, Mr. President."

"In the process? Is this going to be a long process in your estimation?"

Forsyth felt the tension rising in the cramped train car. "No, sir, Mr. President."

The president emitted a menacing sigh. He sat

back in his chair. "Well, now, let's see. "Your Majesty.'" Forsyth realized that that was his cue and quickly dipped a quill into the well in order to set down the president's response.

"I'm speaking to a nine-year-old?"

"Yes, sir."

Van Buren sighed again. "Your Majesty, if I were king of America, I could make this matter disappear as quickly as you desire. However, my hand is stayed by the Constitution of these United States. I shall not speak here to the wisdom of this document. Only to its power over me. Nevertheless, Your Majesty should expect her property to be delivered into the hands of her trusted servant, Señor, ah . . . what's his name?"

"Calderon," Hammond supplied.

"Calderon, within the month or so it will take for this drama to play itself out." He was just about to consider the matter closed when he said aloud a thought he'd just had. "Shall we tell her it's a farce?"

Hammond smiled. "I should pass over the obvious."

The president nodded and continued with his dictation. "Be assured that I shall honor all applicable treaties between our two countries. Be further assured that I recognize the importance of our trade agreements you so kindly refer to in your letter."

12

To Court, Finally

It was still dark on the day when Lewis Tappan, along with Joadson and other abolitionists, arrived with a wagonful of clothes for the captives. They passed among them, passing out clothes. They held up shirts and pants alongside bemused Africans, who were quite interested in the manner and style of these clothes. Of course, they had little experience with such nonfunctional gear. But the colors and the way in which the white people seemed to think it was so generous of them to be able to give clothes away made the activity entertaining. But there were limits. They would not wear shoes. What purpose did they have anyway? Fala loved the feel of earth under his feet. As did Cinque and Yamba and Buakei. As did they all.

And then they were chained again and led out of the prison, marching in a tight formation in their new clothes—clean sack-cloth shirts and cotton pants. As they moved along the street, small groups of citizens jeered them. The Africans could understand very little of what was being said, but they knew it wasn't entirely welcoming. Although there were also groups of abolitionists jeering at those who jeered the Africans.

"What is it? Do they think we want to stay here?"

"No. They want to kill us just because we wanted to go home."

"We should have killed all of them."

"Look how ugly they are."

Cinque was at the back of the group, with Buakei. As he watched the screaming crowds, he noticed a cluster of the same black-robed missionaries he'd seen outside the prison. He nudged Buakei. "Look, it's those miserable-looking people again."

Buakei smiled at him. They both watched the missionaries take up position at the entrance to the courthouse. There they extended Bibles to the blacks as if simply touching the book that held the word of their God would have some effect. But none of the Africans would touch the books. So the missionaries began grabbing at their hands.

"God's blessing on you this morning," someone said to Yamba, who was just ahead of Cinque. A Bible was shoved at him.

"I'm not afraid of you, witch, or your medicine."

"Yes, put your hand on this book and we'll pray for you."

To which Yamba, in an attempt to show courage, snatched the Bible out of the woman's hands and carried it into the courtroom. Cinque and Buakei chuckled at Yamba's aggressive nature. They saw the missionary's eyes light up when Yamba took the Bible.

They were led into the courtroom and directed to three long benches. Cinque ended up in the first bench just behind Baldwin. Baldwin turned around to survey his clients. "Who gave them clothes?"

Tappan, who sat next to him, said, "I did."

"That doesn't help me at all." Baldwin turned to the papers in front of him.

People continued to file into the courtroom. The prosecutors were just arriving. Then the three girls who had been on the *Amistad,* Teme, Margru, and Kahne were escorted in by Mrs. Pendleton. They were completely transformed. Each one wore a white dress. Each one clopped along in new shoes.

Baldwin looked up as the bailiff called, "All rise," and Judge Judson, the same magistrate who had arraigned them, walked into the courtroom. The room became instantly quiet as Judge Judson settled himself behind the bench.

District Attorney Holabird began his opening statement with a dramatic flair that captivated everyone, including the defendants, who still understood nothing about the proceedings.

"And then, in the quietude of night," District Attorney Holabird said, setting the scene of that fateful night. "After the Spaniards had tended their vespers and were deep in virtuous sleep, the savages broke loose their collars and stole like creatures of prey onto the deck where they fell upon the unsuspecting crew with these sabers and cane knives." He walked to a table and passed his hand over the seized weaponry. He picked up a saber and continued talking.

"I cannot overstate the inhumanity of their acts. The savagery. The blood lust. Unsated by the mere deaths of their victims, they went on to mutilate at least one of them. To dismember him, the simple cook, a Creole." He stopped and paused for effect. "By his own kind."

Buakei whispered to Cinque, "Have you figured out who he is?"

"An adviser of some kind. Maybe theirs," he said, nodding in the direction of Lieutenants Meade and Gedney.

The district attorney let the saber fall to the table. When it hit, there was a clatter. "But for the bravery of Señors Ruiz and Montes, who fought their way to the stern and steered the *Amistad* to these shores—under constant threat of like fate of their doomed crewmates—we might never have known of this massacre. This bloodbath. But for their bravery, these villains most certainly would have escaped justice. But they have not." He paused again. "They've not."

Holabird returned to his seat. Baldwin, in contrast, looked unprepared. He lacked the dramatic vision that Holabird had used to mesmerize the courtroom.

Cinque leaned closer to Buakei and gestured toward Baldwin. "I have a horrible feeling he talks for us."

Baldwin walked up to the jury box. He looked rather disheveled.

"Do you know the difference between a cow and a cabbage? A brick and a bear? Well, the Spanish Government hopes you don't have a whole lot more common sense than that. And I'll tell you why. This case isn't about murder or mayhem or massacres. It's not about anything that dramatic. It's about knowing the difference between here and there. I want to show you something." He turned his back on the jury and walked over to Fala.

"Open your mouth." Fala just looked at him. "Of course, he doesn't know what I'm saying because he doesn't speak English. Let's try this, *abierta la boca*. Doesn't understand Spanish either, I guess. I thought he was born on a Cuban plantation. That's what they're all saying."

It was an important point. If the defendants were actually born on Cuban plantations, as Ruiz and Montes contended, then they were indeed slaves and the property of the Spaniards. But if Baldwin could prove that they couldn't speak Spanish and were obviously not born into slavery, then it would go a long way to proving that they had been illegally held. It was a dicey tactic, but Baldwin understood the issues of ownership very well.

"Perhaps he simply doesn't like you, Mr. Baldwin," District Attorney Holabird interrupted.

"He wouldn't be the first, Mr. Holabird," Baldwin quickly rejoined.

Then Baldwin grabbed Fala's mouth, palm at the chin, The thumb on one side and four fingers on the other. He squeezed and roughly parted Fala's lips. He had no idea how fierce a man could be when he was being humiliated this way. If it weren't for the chains, Baldwin would have had to deal with Fala's wrath.

When Fala's teeth were visible, like little spikes, you could feel the shudder that rippled through the jury box. Some even unconsciously brought their hands up as if to soften the image of Fala.

"Did you learn this on a Cuban plantation? This decorative effect?" Baldwin asked.

Fala couldn't believe what was happening. If he could've, he'd have broken this white man's neck. But instead, he just glared at him and silently dared him to remove the chains.

But Baldwin unceremoniously dismissed Fala and approached another African, Kinnah. "Stand up," he said firmly in English and then again in Spanish.

But Kinnah didn't move. Baldwin was now engaged in a drama of his own. "Stand up," he said again, with a grand, sweeping gesture of his arms.

Kinnah stood up. Baldwin pointed to the six scarred lines carved into his cheeks, three on each side. "What's this? Some kind of Cuban initation adornment?" Now Kinnah felt stupid. He'd stood up because he could see clearly that that was what the white man wanted him to do.

District Attorney Holabird slowly and noisily stood up. "Your Honor, I think Mr. Baldwin is trying to tell us that these markings indicate place of origin. In fact, they do not. These and countless other primitive . . . uh . . . embellishments are handed down among slaves from generation to generation. The way we hand down family heirlooms. Regardless of where we . . . or they are born and raised. Indeed, Mr. Baldwin, if you'd like, I'd be happy to go out into the streets of New Haven right now, returning five minutes hence with half a dozen American Negroes bearing even more bizarre scars on their bodies."

"Bring me back one with those teeth while you're at it." Baldwin pointed at Fala.

"Your Honor—" Holabird tried to continue.

But Baldwin cut him off, "Your Honor, these Africans don't belong to the Queen of Spain. Or Cuba. Or—"

"You have no proof they are not." The district attorney could feel some of his influence dissipate.

Baldwin again turned to Kinnah. "What's your name? What's your name? Speak up. I asked you a question."

José Ruiz, who had been sitting in the gallery, waiting for his opportunity seized upon it now, "His name is José," he said rising.

"Ah, Señor Ruiz. The so-called owner of these so-called slaves has spoken. Thank you, sir." And then to Kinnah, "José? That's your name is it?" He then turned his attention to Yamba. "What about his one?"

Ruiz had prepared for this quiz. "Bernardo."

"Bernardo? Of course. That suits him." And then, Baldwin, now at the height of his confidence, sensed the fear that emanated not only from Holabird, but also from the Spaniard. So he asked Yamba, in Spanish, to say, "My name is Bernardo."

Yamba just stared at him.

"I know more Spanish and I was born in Philadelphia."

"Your Honor"—District Attorney Holabird asserted himself—"on Spanish plantations, slaves always choose to live surrounded by their own ways and simple languages. Pray tell, what need they know of Spanish? 'Fetch'? 'Stop'? 'Carry'? Ofttimes, gestures suffice for slaves as they do for any beast of burden."

Joadson felt the sting of the district attorney's words. What did he know about slaves? About what they needed. About what sufficed for them. He had just stated what the fight to end slavery was all about.

Ruiz's attorney jumped from his seat, "Your Honor, I represent the interests of Señors Ruiz and Montes."

"I remember you." Judge Judson sighed weakly.

"This is a bill of sale," he said, waving a document. "Issued in Havana for the purchase of slaves."

"I remember that, too. . . ."

"On it, in addition to the amounts paid for each, are their names. José, Bernardo, Paco, and so on. On behalf of my clients, I present this document to the court."

While this was going on, Cinque had sat there trying to discern what qualities Baldwin had which made him the right one to defend them. And the one thing that stuck with him was the young white man's irreverence. He seemed so confident. Besides Cinque had caught on to Baldwin's method about discerning their origins and it made sense to him.

The judge accepted the bill of sale and took a cursory look at it. He then passed it over to the jury members for their review. "Mr. Baldwin, you've proffered to this court this morning, a good deal of—I'll be kind—ah, circumstantial evidence. Have you, in addition, anything, say, on the order of actual documentation which might refute this one and in so doing more compellingly support your claims?"

Baldwin stared at Judson for a second before saying, "I'm sure I could manufacture some as easily as they have, Your Honor. If that would suffice."

Judge Judson warned him with a long sharp stare. "What you're saying then is, you don't. Is that correct?"

But Baldwin was committed to a strategy which played with the edges of decorum. "I have them," he said definitively. He meant the Africans themselves. They were his evidence.

"I'm afraid that does not impress me."

And all Baldwin could think as he went to sit down was, *What exactly* will *impress you?*

Later that morning Baldwin stood outside the courtroom with Ted Joadson. At the moment he was thinking about the list of names, the bill of sale. "Manuel, Bernardo, Paco."

"I thought you did quite well." Joadson knew that the task before Baldwin was difficult.

"You do?"

"Much better than I expected, to be honest."

"Well, thank you. I think."

Joadson's voice was rich, full of melody even when he spoke in casual conversation. "Although I was concerned for a moment you might have forgotten this is just a case like any other," he teased. He had truly been impressed by Baldwin's performance. Suddenly he hadn't seemed so shallow and expedient.

"You needn't worry about that."

"That's good."

Both men fell silent when they heard the rattling of chains as the captives were led out of the courtroom.

As Cinque passed, he said in Mende, "I know what you're trying to say."

Baldwin didn't understand what Cinque had said, but he did feel the power that came from him. Baldwin took a step back and quickly measured Cinque. He looked at the penetrating eyes. The chiseled face. Intensity—Cinque was the essence of intensity.

And the tall African continued. "I need to speak with you. I know what you're trying to say." And Cinque did *think* he understood Baldwin's approach. It was in the way the young white man gestured. He *felt* that Baldwin was trying to say that no one owned them. And that was the truth. No one did. No one but themselves. But there was no language between them other than these feelings. And then he was dragged away with the others, the sound of chains in his ears.

As Baldwin watched the Africans being led away, he turned to Joadson and asked, "What was that?"

But Joadson had no idea.

13
Making Contact

"An elephant never tires of carrying its tusk."

Baldwin couldn't get Cinque's voice out of his head. The language, the sound of his words were so full of power. And yet there was no comprehension whatsoever. He had no way of being able to interpret that powerful sound into something meaningful. Something that would help him defend them. Help free them.

But if Cinque's voice was what clanged in his head, it was his face that haunted Baldwin. It, too, radiated strength and nobility. More than that however, Cinque's face spoke of the pain and the stress he was encountering. The continual existence in a world that robbed him of his very identity. Here he was, one of the Africans, one of the prisoners. Perhaps the leader of a band of blood-thirsty mutineers. But never, Sengbe Pieh. Never the rice farmer. His face said all of that.

And in a way, Baldwin understood. He didn't know the language, but he did know what he felt.

He had mindlessly wandered into the tavern for his nightly tankard of ale and then taken it outside to sit by the water. Bomoseen, the Abnaki, trudged by, but Baldwin, though he saw him, was too deep in thought to speak.

Suddenly it came to him. If Cinque could communicate that strongly, if he had that much charisma, then he was the one whom Baldwin should be trying to talk to. Maybe he had focused on the wrong African. Maybe Yamba wasn't the one who commanded the most influence and respect. It was Cinque.

Baldwin was fired by this realization. He drained his ale and headed for the prison. With luck they'd let him in.

And with little delay, they did let him in. He found himself standing in the middle of the courtyard, watching Cinque be escorted from his cell in chains. Baldwin studied him. The same gingham shirt, the pantaloons. No shoes. His hands and ankles were manacled, but for a change the neck brace was missing. After he was delivered in front of Baldwin, the guard stepped away.

Baldwin offered his hand. Cinque surprised him by taking it and pulling it to his chest. He held it firm there. Baldwin wanted, even tried to pull it away, but Cinque had a tight hold.

After a second, Baldwin quit struggling and relented. It was then he felt the African's heart. He felt it beating just on the other side of the prisoner's shirt. And what he felt calmed him. What he felt made him realize he could get to know this man.

Cinque finally let his hand go and they both crouched down in the dirt, in the dark, to talk under the watchful eye of a guard some distance away.

"I need to prove where you're from." Baldwin decided to do the simple thing: to say what he wanted. He knew Cinque would never be able to understand him.

And of course, Cinque didn't, but he had his own thoughts. He was engaged in a totally separate process of reasoning. He was finding his own way toward making a meaningful contact with the people who obviously controlled his future. "You want to show them where we're from," he said in Mende. He knew. That had had to be why Baldwin had been screaming all different kinds of languages at them in the courtroom. He had been trying to show that they weren't born slaves. That they had been born free and made into chattel.

"How are you supposed to tell me?" Baldwin couldn't help continuing with this surreal dialog. They were engaged in a discussion in which they could not speak each other's language, but were, in fact, thinking the same thing.

"How can I explain to you where we're from?"

Cinque looked around him. He heard the crickets in the distance, the sounds of the others settling in for the night. The shadows that wrapped themselves in and around the jail cells and spilled out into the courtyard were a part of the audience to their crippled dialog.

And then they were both talking at once. First Baldwin. "Why don't I . . ."

Then Cinque. "Maybe I . . ."

"Excuse me, you should go first."

"I'm sorry, you should talk first."

And these two energies collided in this space and were suddenly silent. Frustrated. After a few breaths, Baldwin tapped on the ground. "This is where I'm from. This"—he gestured about him to mean the surroundings, the town of New Haven—"this is my home."

Baldwin then got hold of an idea. Perhaps he should have thought of it sooner. He grabbed a twig and began drawing in the dirt. He drew a figure to represent the United States. "This is my home," he said again. "Here."

Cinque watched him intently. He wondered about Baldwin. His face had this unique mix of ferocity and sweetness. When they were in the courtroom, even though Cinque knew that Baldwin was fighting for him, he found himself not liking the man. But now he felt something between them. A growing bond of some sort.

Baldwin then drew a smaller outline to suggest

Cuba. "This is Cuba. This is where you were when everyone was killed."

Cinque focused his gaze on the ground between them. He was trying to follow the developing map. Then Baldwin drew a boat near the coast of the Cuba. "The *Amistad*."

Then Baldwin pointed to each shape, and said. "Cuba . . . the *Amistad* . . . here."

Cinque was completely confused. If Baldwin was trying to find out where they were from, he was nowhere near right. He watched Baldwin struggle with his drawing.

"Is this your home?" he said, pointing to Cuba. Cinque just stared at him. This was going nowhere.

And then, as if struck by a certainty, Baldwin drew Africa about eighteen inches away from America. "Africa. This is it, isn't it?"

Cinque was so frustrated he wanted to scream. Did these people know nothing? He got up from his crouch and began walking away, carefully measuring his steps.

Baldwin saw him get up and was immediately defeated. Perhaps it was useless. He'd thought they were close to a breakthrough. But now, with Cinque walking away from him, his anticipation dissipated like dew.

Cinque wasn't leaving, however. He was merely pacing off a true representation of the distance he had traveled to get to "here." After he walked thirty paces, he stopped and turned to face Baldwin, who was stunned when he looked up to see Cinque standing there.

When Cinque knew that Baldwin was staring at him, he said in Mende, "Here. This is my home."

And Baldwin knew then that he'd been right all along. He was right about how the Africans had come to be on board the *Amistad*. He'd also been right that he and Cinque would find a way of communicating. There *was* hope.

Cinque looked at him. They both knew the same thing at the same time. He smiled. There was a chance.

The next day, in the early evening, Baldwin and Joadson hired a boat to take them out to the *Amistad*. "I think you're going to have to find a more definite means of communication than drawing in the dirt," Joadson said to him.

"I know. But it was quite a stunning moment when he stood there all the way on the other side of the prison courtyard. I knew exactly what he was trying to say to me. Indeed, I felt quite stupid, a bit inadequate as an artist."

Joadson smiled. He was glad that Baldwin had asked him along. Perhaps glad was too strong a word. He was surprised at any rate. Baldwin had ignored him for the most part. And Joadson had to admit that no matter how sincere and tireless

Tappan was, there was something about Baldwin that seemed more genuine. Joadson appreciated abolitionists of any color or gender, for that matter. It was the only way slavery would ever be destroyed. Everybody, but particularly every white person, eventually had to come to realize that the idea of owning people was reprehensible and immoral.

Rightly, it was the church movement which had taken the lead, which made the strong case that no good Christian could be a slave owner. And more, that no good Christian could afford to allow slavery to continue. Of course, there were many people who saw themselves as Christians who owned slaves, and others who accepted slavery as a fact of national economic and social life. Indeed, there were people who didn't consider themselves prejudiced, but who saw nothing wrong with slavery. America had always had some kind of servitude or slavery in its fabric. Many Americans could not imagine a life without slavery.

The rise of abolitionism among white citizens was one of the great blessings. Joadson had so much hope for the movement. And he had deep respect for men like Lewis Tappan. But the truth was that Tappan often seemed more preoccupied with his own salvation than the end of slavery. Tappan worked unceasingly to confront the growing specter of white guilt. And sometimes that wore on Joadson's nerves. A man like Baldwin was actually a relief. He was straightforward, and uncomplicated. He just wanted to win this case.

As their boat neared the *Amistad*, Joadson and Baldwin gazed upon the storied ship. It looked even worse than they would have imagined. It was dented and rotting. The wood topside was drying and had been without care. The black paint on its hull, which had made it noticed and mythologized out on the ocean, was now peeling off in wide black ribbons.

But there was another boat leaving the gangway and heading back to shore. As the boats passed each other, Baldwin realized it was Ruiz and Montes. They were in an obvious argument, though neither Joadson nor Baldwin could hear what the subject was. And then they were alongside the *Amistad*, their boat banging against a hemp fender.

Baldwin handed the search warrant to the naval guard. "This is a court order granting us permission to board and search the vessel for evidential purposes."

As the guard read the orders, Baldwin asked him, "What did those two want?"

"To come aboard. I informed them they needed to obtain one of these." He said and handed back the papers. "An authentic one."

Baldwin nodded and motioned Joadson aboard. "Aren't you coming?"

Joadson hadn't thought about it before, but this was not the easiest decision. He knew, even if no one else seemed willing to admit it, that the *Amistad* was a slave ship. It was the symbol of everything that stood against being black in America. It was why America had any blacks in the first place. It was an emotional moment for him. He took a long moment and a deep breath and climbed aboard.

They walked together about the deck. They noted the weapons and the various campsites of the Africans, and the pile of chains in the middle of the main deck. At amidships, Baldwin turned aft and wandered in the direction of the helm. The sun had slipped away and now Baldwin held a lamp over a navigational chart. The paper was worn and thin. It made him think that it would fall apart at any moment. He wasn't sure what he was looking for precisely, but he felt that something on the ship might prove that its passengers were actually African-born people who had been illegally enslaved. He continued going through all of the charts and papers. One thing was clear and that was that Ruiz and Montes had told the truth about their intended route. The maps clearly showed them leaving Havana on a charted course to Principe.

In the meantime, Joadson had wandered into

the slave decks. It was dreadfully dark and stifling. The ship groaned and there was the gentle
sloshing of the water against the hull. But, in a
way, there was an eery stillness there. He held his
lantern close to the hull where he could see the
dried bloodstains that were splattered against the
wooden planks. He felt almost dizzy. It was as
though the pain of all the people who had been
jammed in these holds on the many voyages of
the *Amistad* still permeated the air with a acrid,
toxic, throat-choking thickness.

Then he saw something lying on the deck. It
was a small charm. He didn't know it, but it was
Cinque's: The same one that was given to him by
Tafe.

Baldwin entered the cramped hold from the
other end, his lantern swinging the shadows
across the bulkheads. He stopped and stared at
Joadson, who was studying the charm. After a
second, he continued his approach, but there was
something slick on the deck there. He slipped,
dropped his lamp, and hit the deck with a clatter.

The racket startled Joadson so much, he
dropped his lantern, too. Then they were both
there. On the slave decks. In the dark. It frightened Joadson beyond self-control. He was petrified. "Mr. Baldwin?"

"It's me, Joadson."

"Light the lamp."

"I'm trying." Baldwin had been groping on his

hands and knees to find his lantern. And then he had to find a match. He finally got the lamp relit. "There. Are you all right?"

"Yes."

By the light of his lantern, Baldwin's eyes were drawn instantly to another object which he could see wedged between the timbers. It was the pouch that Ruiz had slid between the planks above, just before the *Amistad* was intercepted by the U.S. Navy. In that pouch were the papers that would turn the case in favor of the Africans. He was sure of it.

14
To Win; To Lose

"No one ever ponders his own first name."

"These papers, and I shall ask you to examine them, are portions of a ship's manifest I retrieved from the *Amistad* yesterday eve. I should say 'ferreted' because, in fact, they'd been hidden and came to light, literally, as I relit a lantern on the slave decks which lay beneath the stern. They'd obviously slipped through the wood and fallen there. At first glance perhaps, these papers should appear to bolster the prosecution's case. They list cargo. Cargo bearing the very Spanish names. Mr. Ruiz and Mr. Montes insist they represent my clients. But, lo . . . this is not the manifest of the *Amistad* at all. Look. This is part of the cargo manifest of a Portuguese vessel. The notorious transatlantic slave ship. The *Tecora*."

The courtroom was immediately disrupted with the shuffling of papers and the traveling whispers that rippled through the prosecution table and the gallery behind them. Even Cinque could tell that Baldwin had made an important point. And Montes had turned to Ruiz with a look of absolute terror and anger. He could have hidden those papers better.

"The *Tecora*, and I can bring in as many witnesses as you wish, Mr. Holabird, to corroborate this, is known to ply its trade primarily off the coast of West Africa. The Ivory Coast. Sierra Leone." He then turned to the jury. "I know what you're thinking. 'Sierra Leone is a Protectorate of the British Crown. Slavery is outlawed there. Its principal port, in fact, has been rechristened Freetown, hasn't it?' How then can the Portuguese flag-flying *Tecora* engage in the slave trade in these waters? I'll tell you how. In a word. Illegally."

Judge Judson looked now to the prosecutors. He seemed a bit more skeptical of them. If they knew the entire affair was essentially just the illegal transport of slaves, it would be a different case than what it had seemed at first.

"Whatever these men say from this point on," Baldwin continued, pointing to Ruiz and Montes, "clearly matters not, because this proves them liars."

Baldwin stepped forward and handed the judge the papers he'd found. "My clients' journey did not begin in Havana as they claim and keep claiming more and more emphatically. It began much, much further away." He paused and caught Cinque's gaze. He held it there. And then continued. "These men and women are not slaves. Are not property. And never have been. They were kidnapped from their homes in Africa, rose up against their kidnappers, as I dare say you or I would if we had half their courage, and sit before you now, still in chains, asking you to render judgment. I have no doubt that judgment will be fair." Baldwin concluded his statement with dramatic finality, and then returned to his chair.

After Judge Judson adjourned, the corridor outside the courtroom was jammed. The spectators, the attorneys, and the prisoners were for a moment all trapped in the passageway. Baldwin found Cinque's eyes as the prisoners were led from the courtroom and nodded to him. District Attorney Holabird came out shortly after and had to push past the very people he sought to keep in chains.

Lewis Tappan emerged from the crowd and rushed up to Baldwin with his hand extended. "I underestimated you, sir," he said as he vigorously shook Baldwin's hand.

Even while Tappan pumped his arm, Baldwin looked at Joadson and smiled. "I should take that as a compliment."

"You should indeed, sir. You've done it, I think.

I can't imagine this now not reaching a favorable conclusion." Tappan was nearly giddy.

Baldwin understood Tappan's glee. What he had done was slowly sinking in. He had to admit, he was quite satisfied himself. He'd stepped before a hostile court and proven his point. But at that moment, out of the crowd burst a man who, without saying a word, hit Baldwin across the side of the head and bolted away.

Baldwin screamed in pain as he grabbed Tappan's shoulder to keep from falling. Joadson immediately took after the assailant. He followed the man through the crowds and into the street. But there he lost contact, and the man slipped into the flow of pedestrians all about.

Joadson wedged back through the crowd that had gathered around Baldwin. Tappan had moved Baldwin to a staircase.

"Am I bleeding?" Baldwin asked as he looked at his hand, which showed no blood.

"Let me see." Tappan touched his head.

"Gently."

Joadson looked at Baldwin and said, "He got away."

Baldwin looked at him with bewilderment. "What did I do to deserve that?"

For the first time Joadson saw how innocent Baldwin really was. "You took the case, Mr. Baldwin. It's just that simple."

The implications of the *Amistad* case continued to grow. In Washington, President Van Buren had received and read a letter from Queen Victoria, herself only a few years older than Queen Isabella II of Spain, in which she had politely laid claim to "a group of British subjects that are at present in detention in a New Haven prison." Now he sat with his personal secretary, Leder Hammond, and the Secretary of State, John Forsyth, in the president's office developing a strategy to deal with the *Amistad* affair.

"I'm not about to bend to the will of some pubescent queen. Either of them," the president said with a strained smile.

"Forget about them, they're unimportant." Hammond rushed to his support.

When President Van Buren thought about Isabella in particular, he couldn't help saying, *"Prepubescent."*

"What you need to concern yourself with, Mr. President, is what this matter means here. Not an ocean away."

"I wish someone would tell me what it means. You yourself, Leder, said it was meaningless."

Hammond paused awkwardly and turned to Forsyth. "Not anymore, Mr. President. Not anymore."

Forsyth knew it was his turn to talk. "I've received a parade of visits from our Southern senator friends, anxious for us to understand exactly what this case means." He leaned forward. "If the Africans are executed, the abolitionists will certainly make good use of it and yes, they will make some converts. If, on the other hand, they are freed, if that happens, the Southern states, we are to be assured, will so ally themselves against you that . . . that you can forget about reelection." He'd put it as directly as he knew how. Van Buren needed to know this was no longer a small matter.

As one of Van Buren's chief advisers and a cabinet member, John Forsyth's political future was strongly connected to the president's reelection in 1840. Therefore, it was in Forsyth's best interest to assure that the *Amistad* case was dealt with expeditiously and with as little negative political reaction as possible. But it was obvious that there was already a political debt being incurred to the slave-owning states.

He had to explain to the president that they had to tread relatively lightly because the federal executive branch could not legally meddle with the decisions of a state-level judiciary. Still, he was as involved as the administration could afford for him to be.

Van Buren was stunned. "Over this?"

"It's worse than that."

"Worse? How could it be worse?"

"In addition to inspiring uprisings in every

state by American Negroes, it could take us all one long step closer to civil war."

To Van Buren's way of thinking, this was bordering on the absurd. Who cared about a group of Africans who'd washed up on shore out of a storm? Who cared?

"All is not lost." Forsyth tried to act a little more confident. "Yes, the judge appears disposed toward freeing them. But judges can be removed."

Without thinking, Van Buren felt a flash of optimism. "They can?"

"He could be prevailed upon to recuse himself for any number of reasons." Forsyth waited for the president to acknowledge that he understood, which he eventually did. And then Forsyth continued. "With that in mind, I've taken the liberty of exploring possible replacements, and have found one I strongly believe to be, ah, better."

Van Buren fingered his white mutton chops, "Well . . ."

"His name is Bertrand Coglin, Judge Bertrand Coglin, sir. He's young, which means he has a career before him rather than behind. Which means he's yet to feel the hankering for magnanimous last gestures for the sake of posterity." He took a sip from his glass. "And he is monumentally insecure, particularly about his Catholic heritage."

That caught Van Buren's attention. A Catholic judge? "He's Catholic?"

"His grandfather was Catholic, which young Mr. Coglin has striven, all his days, to keep quiet."

"I see." The president did see exactly what Forsyth was proposing. There was no fighting it, he needed the Southern vote. He especially needed the support of the slave owners. "Well, let's get him out here for a talk, shall we?"

Hammond, who had listened to the conversation intently, answered, "Yes, Mr. President."

And so the *Amistad* case became even more complex. Not only were Spain and England making claims, along with the arresting officers, but the obvious slave runners, Ruiz and Montes, wanted the ship and its captives back. Now, partly to ensure reelection, the President of the United States was manipulating judicial assignments in order to influence the outcome.

Not many days later, a courier from the court appeared at Baldwin's office. Joadson was there as he had been more and more. He felt there was something he could learn from the young barrister. And perhaps he symbolized something to Baldwin. Something that Baldwin hadn't spent enough time thinking about—Joadson represented the truth that a black man could be intelligent, aggressive, and influential. It'd been too easy for most ambitious young white men to ignore the plight of America's black citizens.

Baldwin took the letter from the courier. As he fumbled with the envelope, the farmer who'd been there earlier with his goats came rushing in, this time leading a pig. "Mr. Baldwin," he said with short breath.

Without looking up from the letter, Baldwin motioned for silence with an upraised hand. But the farmer was much too excited to comply. "Mr. Baldwin, you did it. We won. The land between the pond and the trees is mine."

But Baldwin was totally consumed by the letter. It was not good. The *Amistad* case would have to be tried again. With a new judge. It was obviously coming from the highest positions of power. The case had been won. He'd fought for the freedom of the Africans and now the state was trying to take that away.

The farmer couldn't help his enthusiasm. "Of course, I can't pay you. But in gratitude, I want you to have my best sow."

Baldwin heard him, but he had lost his vision. He couldn't believe they were doing this. He crumpled the letter in his hands. He turned and stared at Joadson. He looked into the black man's eyes. Suddenly he couldn't look into a black person's eyes without seeing the struggle that had been going on all around him. He grabbed and threw his desk lamp. It shattered against the wall.

The pig squealed and ran for cover. Then Baldwin flung a box of papers across the room.

Joadson considered it his duty to try something extraordinary. That was why he'd insisted Tappan get him an invitation to visit with John Quincy Adams. He felt the former president was the only one with the knowledge, influence, and respect to win the battle of public opinion. It was the large indifference to slavery that was embedded in the American psyche that had to be fought against for the *Amistad* case to be fairly adjudicated.

He'd gotten the invitation and was now clattering along a road leading up to Adams's stately farmhouse. He was greeted by black servants and led to the library. He couldn't help seeing the frozen stares that came from the black faces and white faces of those in the house.

The former president was standing over a rather sickly potted plant. It was actually the Blush Noisette rose that had rooted from the cutting he taken from the Congressional Gardens the first time Joadson had met him. He heard Joadson come in, but continued his careful pruning. "I've been reading in the papers and not just yours, Mr. Joadson, the continuing saga of the *Amistad*. Real papers."

"Real papers, yes." Joadson smiled.

"Bad luck, this last unfolding chapter. What to do now, eh?"

Joadson watched Adams's back. He wondered if the president would turn and face him or would their entire conversation be held this way. "That is precisely why I've come to Massachusetts and imposed on you, Mr. President."

"No imposition, really." He paused. "How's the lawyer taking the news?"

"In stride." Joadson wanted to laugh, but kept himself under total control. Even a free black man had to discharge his personality in small portions. "The thing is, he did everything right. He proved the case."

"Did he?"

"Yes. Surprisingly, he did."

Adams finished with the rose and turned his attention to a hearty peach-colored lily. "Well, I guess he'll just have to do it again then, won't he? Like most things, it should be easier the second time around."

Joadson tried to retain his control, though the white-haired patriarch tried his patience. "I'm afraid, at this point, it doesn't matter what he does. Rumor has it our new judge was handpicked by Van Buren himself."

Adams had been in the White House. He knew the power that rested there. "No."

Joadson could tell from the tone of Adams's voice that he thought he should have guessed as

The schooner *La Amistad*. The ship was en route from Havana, destined for Puerto Principe on the southern part of the island—a trip that should have taken two days. The schooner was on its third night of rough seas when Cinque freed himself and then the other captives.

In the hold of the slave ship.

Cinque tells Ruiz to sail east, toward the sun,
back to Africa. Fala, in the background, performs
his death wish chant.

Cinque argues with Yamba about the fate
of Montes and Ruiz.

Maseray and the children in prison, before
Mrs. Pendleton takes them to become "her girls."

Cinque waits apprehensively in his cell.

Cinque leads a prison yard riot, demanding
to bury his African brother Fala in the traditions
of their homeland.

An African wears a turban made from ransacked cargo.

Cinque pulls Baldwin's hand to his chest, holding it against his heart.

The former slave Joadson pauses in the courtroom, weary of all the failed arguments for freedom for his brothers.

In the greenhouse, Adams sees for himself the humanity and dignity of the African Cinque, who examines a violet tenderly.

Cinque speaks in the courtroom: "Give us free!"

Baldwin presents prosecutor Holabird with the documents he has found hidden on the *Amistad* from the earlier journey of the *Tecora*.

Cinque, ready to sail home.

much. "I suppose I am embarrassed to admit I was under the misconception that the judicial and executive branches were separate."

"No more than these, Mr. Joadson." Adams held two leaves up in his hand. Joadson saw that the two leaves were connected to one stem. That was his point. Joadson understood him perfectly.

"If it were you trying the case . . ."

"It isn't I, thank God for that."

"If it were you, what would you do?"

Finally Adams turned around and fully faced Joadson. "When I was an attorney, a long time ago, young man, I realized after much trial and error that in a courtroom whoever tells the best story wins. In un-lawyerlike fashion, I give you that scrap of wisdom free of charge." Both men were silent for a time before Adams asked as an afterthought, "What *is* their story by the way?"

Joadson thought for a moment and said, "They're . . . they're from West Africa."

"No. What's their *story*?"

Joadson shrugged. He really didn't know their story.

"Mr. Joadson, you're from where originally?"

"Georgia."

"Georgia? Does that pretty much sum up what you are? A Georgian? Is that your story? No. You're an ex-slave who has devoted his life to the abolition of slavery, overcoming great obstacles and hardships along the way, I imagine. That's your story isn't it?" He paused. He could see that Joadson was surprised by his statement, but it needed to be said. Baldwin was missing the point and so was Joadson.

"You and this so-called lawyer have proven you know *what* they are: They're Africans. Congratulations. Now, what you don't know and, as far as I can tell, haven't bothered in the least to find out is *who* they are."

Joadson stood there and felt a chill ripple through his body. It was true. Baldwin didn't know and neither did he. Who were they? And how would they find out?

15
The Power

"It is little drops that flood a river."

In New Haven a light rain fell, turning the vibrant bayside town into a gray muddiness. What wasn't brick or stone quickly turned to mud. This was especially true in the prison courtyard, where it seemed the ground was never dry long enough to completely rid itself of mud. It had been raining all afternoon and now, in the early hours of darkness, a gentle mist flurried. In the jailer's quarters, Colonel Pendleton sat reading a book, occasionally nodding his approval at his wife, who attempted to teach the three African girls a hymn she was playing on the piano. The girls mouthed an occasional word but, for the most part, they hummed along to Mrs. Pendleton's spirited playing.

Outside, in the general prison area, the music mixed with the rain and the increasing chill of fall in New England. Yamba had become consumed with the Bible he'd gotten from the missionaries. He was especially fascinated by the illustrations, of which there were many.

In another cell, Buakei and Cinque spoke quietly. "If things are going as well as you thought, why are we still here?" Buakei, like nearly everyone else, was becoming increasingly frustrated.

"Maybe I was wrong. Maybe I don't know anything." As usual, Cinque was a reluctant leader. He questioned his own courage. He questioned his own wisdom. He'd tried to make the best decisions, to accept to a certain degree the authority that many of the Mende and indeed some of the others gave to him. They'd tried to escape the terror of the slavers and ended up in jail.

More and more, Cinque wondered whether he could trust the justice system of the white man to help him go back home. Everything that had happened, happened because they were trying to go back home. Cinque often wondered what it would be like to go back to the moment before he was kidnapped. That was the thing. The death of the crew of the *Amistad* had been the price of the ticket to get home. Couldn't the white men in their fancy halls of justice see that?

How would they get out of this peril they faced? Cinque thought about the lion he'd killed. Its eyes. It had looked him in the eye and dared him to be anything but brave. Cinque had fooled the lion and himself. In the end he'd done the right thing. In the end he had been brave. He hoped that somehow he would find the right magic to free them all from the madness they were slowly being consumed by.

As he sat thinking, his eyes settled on Fala, who was across the yard, curled into a ball, shivering as he tried to sleep. He had a thin blanket over him, but it was obviously not enough. Cinque stood and grabbed his own blanket and walked toward Fala. He knew that technically Fala was staying with the Temne, which meant that he would have had to cross their "territory." Instead, he walked to the Temne area and handed the blanket to a guard there. "Give this to the Kissi."

The guard took the blanket and, instead of giving it to Fala, handed it to Yamba.

"I said the Kissi." Cinque couldn't believe that the guard would do that. What was the harm in giving Fala the blanket?

Yamba examined the blanket and then said to Cinque, "I heard you." Yet he made no move to give it up to Fala. Instead, he pulled it over the blanket he was already using and went back to reading his Bible.

"Pass the blanket on."

"Be quiet. I'm trying to read."

Cinque was stunned by this blatant show of disrespect. He had felt it growing between them since back on the *Amistad*. Cinque knew it had something to do with the way Baldwin was spending so much time with him. After all, Baldwin had approached Yamba first. It wasn't Cinque's fault that he and Baldwin seemed to have a special connection. And for sure, Fala shouldn't have to suffer because of it.

Cinque grabbed an empty brass piss pot, a necessary accouterment of imprisonment, and began clanging it along the bars of the cell. Yamba tried to ignore it, but Cinque kept at it. The guards began to get a little nervous. Finally Yamba leaped up from his cot and screamed at Cinque, "All right! You ignorant shrieking Mende!" He then balled up the blanket, walked over to Fala, and threw it on top of him.

Fala seemed to be getting sicker. He was sweating and shivering at the same time. He looked up weakly and said, "Thank you."

As Yamba returned to his cot, he glared at Cinque. "You are not the 'big man' here. Don't forget that."

Cinque knew then that he had been right in sensing the rising tension between himself and Yamba. The Temne was obviously feeling overlooked and was angry.

During this squabble between the Africans, Baldwin was in his office, learning the names of the various tribes that were being held together. Professor Gibbs had returned with a little more information than he had the first time they had visited the prison. Joadson was there as well, listening as Gibbs talked about the Sherbro, the Fula, and the Mende.

Gibbs had a slate with the names of the tribes at the top. Under each one were ten short words.

"Now let's do Mende. 'One' is *eta*, 'two' is *fili*, 'three' is *kiauwa*, then *naeni*."

Both Baldwin and Joadson repeated the lesson back to Gibbs. Gibbs had hit upon a novel idea. He thought that if they covered the waterfront counting in Mende or Sherbro, they might get lucky and find someone who spoke one of the languages.

After they'd spent most of the evening with their studies, Baldwin and Joadson headed for the wharf. There they split up and began walking along the wharf counting in Mende. They looked particularly for black people—sailors, citizens, and slaves. They walked near groups of people who were just standing around or leaving a ship. At each opportunity, they would begin counting, hoping someone would understand them.

They struck quite the image. Even though they didn't approach people as a team, it was obvious that they were together. A black man in a suit traveling with a young, bespectacled white man, both muttering strange words. People backed away from them. Stared at them. But no one acted as if the words they were saying had meaning.

Eventually, feeling a little defeated, they made

AMISTAD

their way to the Harbor Tavern. As usual, it was crowded, noisy, and thick with smoke. They continued their search by wandering around the tables, counting aloud in the various languages.

Baldwin walked by a table at which a young black man dressed in a British naval uniform sat drinking with a group of his mates and his commanding officer. The young man thought he heard someone speaking in Mende, but was sure he'd only thought it. It had been years since he'd heard his native tongue, especially spoken in such an infantile way.

Then Joadson came by, repeating the same numbers. It was then that the man was sure that he was hearing Mende.

He ran Joadson down. "Excuse me, what are you doing?"

Joadson looked at the black man and smiled. "Do you understand what I'm saying?"

"You're counting, aren't you?" He paused. "Are you Mende?"

Joadson stopped walking and turned fully to face him, "No, sir, but if you speak the Mende language, I'm very very happy to make your acquaintance."

"The name's Covey, mate, James Covey," the man said as he let Joadson lead him to a table. Baldwin quickly joined them. Covey had also invited his commanding officer to the table. Baldwin and Joadson looked at each other with rising expectations. This was a very important find. They learned that the man was Ensign James Covey of the British Royal Navy. The ensign was nineteen years old and had been captured much the same as the other Africans from near the coast of West Africa. Luckily though, his slave ship had been captured by the British navy and its slaves had been freed and returned to Africa. Covey had quickly befriended a sailor who taught him English and then had chosen to join Her Majesty's navy. Now he was attached to a ship that happened to be in port.

It didn't take much to convince Covey to agree to meet them at the prison the next day. Covey's captain was surprisingly interested in encouraging Covey's cooperation. The story of the *Amistad* and the trials connected with it were already legendary, though Covey didn't need much encouragement anyway. These were his brothers and sisters. If he could help them, he would. And it was the nature of his captain to join any fight against slavery.

The next morning Baldwin, Joadson, and Covey met at the gate of the prison. There was a gray and threatening cast to the sky. It had been raining intermittently over the past few days and everything was shrouded by the clouds.

But there was also a tightening crispness in the air as winter began to whisper its entry. As fall ended, there was a gradual, yet ever pressing chilliness that intensified until it erupted in snow and freezing temperatures. And then New Haven, as would all Connecticut and its surrounding territories, began to look as they were meant to. With cloaks of white snow covering the ground and gusting winds that blew over hill and main street.

The only sure-fire antidote, or perhaps complement to winter was the warmth and crackle of a fire in the hearth. In this eastern region of America, the two lived in balance. Cold and fire. Together they created a picture of beauty. Images that had beguiled poets and painters for ages.

As they approached the gates, all three men could hear a series of shouts and threats coming from within. Cinque and nearly all the other prisoners were poised in a standoff with the guards. Off to the side, Yamba stood with two other Temne. It was obvious that Yamba had not yet decided whether he would fight with Cinque or not.

But Cinque suffered no indecision. "We will all die here if you do not listen to me. We will fight you until we all lose our breath!" Cinque screamed in Mende. But the guards had no idea of what he was saying. They just stood there, tension growing in their bodies, their guns loaded and aimed at the Africans.

Cinque swallowed hard. It had once again

reached the point at which he felt he had to assert himself on behalf of his people. All right. They had been kidnapped. Okay. They had been brought across the great ocean in chains and filth. Okay. They had been sold into bondage. They were now in prison for fighting for their own freedom. Okay. But they could not allow these white men and their laws to prevent them from paying the proper respect and honor to their dead. This was not okay.

Baldwin stared in amazement. He couldn't believe the resolute fierceness he saw in the eyes of the men who stood facing the guns. He carefully got close enough to one of the guards to ask, "What happened?"

"Nothing." The guard was obviously both surprised and shaken by the turn of events. None of them really knew why this was happening. "One of them died. We were taking the body out to bury it. What do they want? Do they want to live with it?"

And then Baldwin saw Fala's body. He immediately turned his head to Cinque. He'd seen Cinque's fondness for Fala. In Cinque's face was pure sadness. Baldwin felt it. They all felt it.

Ensign Covey quietly walked up behind him and said, "*They* want to bury him. They have to bury him or his soul will haunt them forever."

Baldwin heard him and understood. Suddenly he knew there was only one way this could end peacefully. He also knew that Covey would be a very important man from now on. He was the lifeline to Cinque and the rest of the captives.

Baldwin turned and went looking for Colonel Pendleton, who was the only one who could resolve this situation. He found the jailer in the cell block, armed with a musket, but immobile. Baldwin could see the fear in his eyes. Covey and Joadson came up behind him. They all saw Pendleton shaking.

"If I were you . . ." Baldwin did not need to finish the sentence, but he did anyway. "If I ran this place, I'd set protocol aside—just this once— and let them bury him."

It took only a heartbeat for Pendleton to nod in agreement. "I was thinking the same thing," he said and left them in silence.

Baldwin, Joadson, and Covey let Pendleton's absence settle in the air around them. The guards eventually retreated to their posts. The prisoners slowly came together in a kind of meeting.

"These tribes," began Covey, "would have nothing to do with each other at home. As little as possible anyway. The Mende consider the Lokko backwards. The Kono say the Fula are thieves. The Sherbro, well, they're hardly worth thinking about at all. They're so honest they're foolish. If a Sherbro finds money, for instance, he almost always gives it back. The Temne are the only ones the Mende have any respect for because of their fighting abilities. But they also hate them for the same reason. They've lost a lot of land to the Temne over the years."

As he'd been talking, the discussion among the tribes had evidently turned into an election of sorts. Covey continued, "The problem here is that none of them truly has the right to perform a burial. None of them is important enough." He stopped talking as Cinque stepped out from his group of Mende, which was the largest of the tribes, and Yamba then emerged from the Temne, the next largest.

Covey lowered his voice, "This should be interesting."

The two men stood in front of the entire group and a kind of election took place as each man stood on the side of the candidate he supported. When everyone had decided, Cinque had won by three votes.

Yamba didn't look particularly pleased with the results and couldn't help saying, "He's going to do this? He's not a chief."

Cinque looked into Yamba's eyes. "I know I'm not." But he knew that he was the one his people had chosen. His life always seemed to be buffeted by the need of those around him to see him as a leader. He knew that his body, his height, his physique, made people think of him as powerful. But there was something else. Something Yamba didn't have. Perhaps it was an unflinching confidence in the power of his ancestors to overcome all obstacles to freedom. He was bound to be free. He didn't want to lead prisoners. He wanted to go home. But in the meantime, if they wanted him to bury Fala, he would do that.

Joadson had watched the scene with pride. He'd never imagined that Africans, his own forefathers, had ever been able to deliberate, to vote. How frightening slavery was that it could obliterate such a memory. Slavery had convinced American blacks that they could not do such things. Indeed, there were people who tried to make the case that slavery was good for black people. That it kept their lives simple and uncomplicated. Just do what we say, when we say, how we say, or we'll . . . Here was proof that all of that was a lie. Black people did not *need* white people to lead them. There was no good in slavery for black people, regardless of who argued otherwise—scholars or philosophers. There were no benefits that accrued to the slaves.

He then watched Cinque wash Fala's body in warm water, which he wrung from rags heated over a fire. Buakei sharpened the end of a stick by rubbing it against a stone wall and then, when it was pointed, he handed it to Cinque. Cinque then lifted one of Fala's hands and made a cut with the stick across the back of it. A slight trace of blood showed where the skin separated.

"There. You'll be recognized when you return," Cinque said as he carefully laid the hand back down and began wrapping Fala's body in cloth.

And later that morning, there was an incredible assemblage of people at the cemetery. It had been like a parade for the fallen Kissi. All of the Africans were there, including the three girls—who were looking more and more American with their new clothes—and Mrs. Pendleton, the guards, a group of missionaries and, of course, the lawyers.

The chanting began with a single voice, but quickly became a complexly woven texture of sound which represented both the tribe and the tribute to the end of a life. Each tribe intoned their own sound, their own prayer. First, the Mende:

Fala, Fala, be accepted in the paradise of the creator.
Yes, Fala, be accepted in a blanket of heaven.

Then the Temne:

One God, One God, God
Prophet Muhammed
Peace and blessing be upon him until the day we die.

The Ibo voice added:

> *Bear it, bear it, bear it,*
> *Bearing it is best.*
> *Whosoever the burdens come upon,*
> *Bearing it is best.*

Cinque's voice reached over the chants. "The unexpected always happens. We did what we could, but our efforts were in vain. The proud warrior, Fala, is dead."

Covey whispered the translation for Baldwin and Joadson. It was like a play. Each group knew what they were supposed to do. Maseray, the young woman, began a long plaintive song. The girls dropped down and began smearing their faces with mud, much to the horror of Mrs. Pendleton.

Cinque knelt by the body and said, "Fala, we've built you a house, but we can't provide you with any money. We haven't any. I apologize." He then climbed into the grave. Buakei joined him there. Fala's body was handed down to them. Cinque then draped his blanket over Fala. The others brought tree branches, which Cinque and Buakei put over the body. Cinque pulled himself up and helped Buakei to the surface. Each of them then took a handful of dirt and dropped it into the grave. Everyone followed suit in the procession.

Cinque stood over the grave. He'd seen too many people die on this journey. People he had barely had a chance to speak with and for whom he had no feelings, and then people like Fala, who had worked their way into his heart. He felt for Fala and wished him well.

16

The Lion Killer

Much of that afternoon was spent with the excitement over Ensign Covey. Most of the captives were overwhelmed that there was finally someone who understood them. Covey, Joadson, and Baldwin took considerable time and care in their conversations. Through much of it, Cinque sat alone, watching.

Later, Baldwin, Covey, and Joadson found Cinque in silent contemplation in a corner of his cell. A guard brought a chair for Baldwin, leaving the two black men to fend for themselves. Covey sat on a crate and Joadson chose to stand.

Covey began speaking in Mende. "My name is Kai Nyagua, and James Covey. I speak Mende and English"—he pointed to Baldwin—"his language. You and he will talk to each other through me."

Cinque stared at him. A Mende with two names and some sort of uniform.

But Covey read Cinque quickly. "The clothes," he said, apologetically.

"And the name," Cinque added.

"I was rescued off a slave ship by the British Navy." He paused. "I never went back."

Cinque nodded, but was still hesitant to trust any of these people too much.

Finally, Baldwin spoke. "A problem has arisen." Covey began his translation back and forth. "The judge we had, who believed, I believe, you should be freed, has been dismissed. A new judge has been called upon to hear the case. This time without a jury."

"How is that possible? Judges can't be replaced." Cinque wondered whether not knowing was better. How could they change judges?

"I can't explain it in any way that would make sense to you, or me, really. Only that it happened." Baldwin took a long pause. What they needed to win only Cinque could provide. "Cinque, I am not a great orator or adviser. I am not a big man in my profession. I don't know that, alone, I can convince this next judge to let you go. I need you to help me. When we return to court, I need you to speak."

Cinque considered the request. "I'm not an adviser of any kind," he said. "I certainly can't speak for the others."

"They say you can. They say you're the 'big man' here."

Cinque couldn't help smiling to himself. So that was what the others had told Covey. They wanted him to speak for them. He was a little surprised, though it seemed at every turn he was the one they chose to lead them.

"I'm not," he said humbly.

Baldwin realized that convincing Cinque to represent all of the Africans might be difficult, but he was not prepared to take "no" for an answer. There were others listening to their conversation. Eyes peered from the surrounding cells. "What's this I hear about a lion?" he said, to change the subject and the mood.

Cinque sighed and looked away.

"They say you alone slew the most terrifying beast anyone has ever seen. It's not true?"

Cinque thought about the story. "It had killed several people. Everyone, including me, was afraid." He began reluctantly to tell the story of how he really did kill a lion. When he was finished, he said, "It was an accident. If I had missed when I threw the rock, no one would be telling you about it now. I'd just be dead. I'm not a big man. Just a lucky one."

"I might agree with you. Except you're forgetting something. The other lion."

Cinque stared blankly.

"The *Amistad*. The insurrection. That, too, was an accident? I hardly think so."

179

"That wasn't bravery. Any man would do the same to get back to his family. You would do it."

Baldwin regarded Cinque's explanation. He wasn't so sure he would have had the courage to go up against an armed crew.

Joadson leaned over and handed him the charm that he had found on the slave decks of the *Amistad*. "Someone said this was yours?"

Cinque couldn't believe it. He thought he'd seen the last of it that night they stormed out of the slave decks and took control of the *Amistad*. "My wife gave this to me . . . to keep me safe." The irony of that simple statement had a sobering effect on him. It had, after all, kept him safe. But he was still a long way from home. He fondled the figure slowly in his hand. And maybe for the first time he felt close to tears. He remembered his wife and missed her so terribly. He missed the sound of her morning song. The strength of her grip.

Baldwin could see the pain in Cinque's eyes and took that opportunity to press forward. "I want you to tell me how you got here."

Cinque looked up at Baldwin. He'd wondered how long it would take before he'd have a chance to tell his story. He'd rehearsed it in his head many times. It was, in fact, the way he went to sleep many nights. He would lie there and see himself leaving his hut and walking to the rice fields, watching the sun smile sweetness over his growing crops. He imagined the overwhelmingly humid heat that wrapped him and his family like the cloth he'd sent Fala to the other side in.

Yes, he was prepared to tell his story.

17
Before He Was Cinque

MENDELAND, WEST AFRICA

"However tall one may grow, one can never grow taller than the hair on one's head."

Sengbe had grown up in Mani, a village populated mostly by rice farmers, of which his father was headman. Mani was governed by King Kalumbo, who lived some distance away. But in truth, this was their country. Their world.

The lives of the Mende and the other tribes in this part of West Africa were relatively simple. They were common, self-sufficient folk who could get what they wanted from the animals they raised and what grew in the earth they tilled.

They were farmers and hunters and garment makers. They were teachers and doctors. There was a village judicial system and a ritual for everything. From birth to death, the Mende would call upon the generosity and wisdom of the ancestors to guide them. Much of their culture was governed by secret tribal organizations, like the Poro for men, and the Sande for women, that regulated and celebrated nearly every significant event in a person's life.

The Mende were brave and capable in battle, but some of the neighboring Temne tribes were considered more formidable. Still, the Mende, as did the other tribes, had to be prepared for confrontations and aggressions. There *had* been occasional wars. The tribes of the region were increasingly more adventurous. There were raids on the village during which food was stolen and sometimes people were captured and spirited away as the spoils of war: slaves.

It was on one of the first days of the planting season that Sengbe was snatched from his life in Mani. This growing season was especially important because he needed his share of the harvest to pay off a rather large debt he had incurred from a Vai tribesman, who was becoming increasingly more impatient.

On this morning Sengbe awoke as usual with the roosters. He carefully tied his *gris-gris*—talismans and charms—on his arms as most Mende men did. Each charm was a connection to the past, to family, ancestors, and the spirits which affected their lives every day. One of Sengbe's favorites had been given to him by his wife. It was a small wooden figure wrapped with a few strands of her hair and their children's. He wore it strapped to his biceps, in a leather pouch that his mother used to wear around her neck. It held the most power and always seemed to lead him out of danger. It was a way of taking his protection with him. Sometimes when he was away from home and he touched her charm, he would hear her voice deep inside his head. There was never a time since they were married that he didn't feel connected to her.

He ate and prepared to walk to his rice farm as he always did. He kissed his wife and each of his children before leaving, which again, he did every morning. And then he left home with a smile on his face and the hope that his ancestors would protect his family.

He had cut a narrow path through the creeping forest which bordered his land on the outskirts of the village. It was a little less than a mile long. The path passed through a dense area of mahogany trees and bushes, and opened into the swampy area where many of the village had their farms. His farm was there as well.

It was a short walk, but one that Sengbe always enjoyed. He loved the feel of the soft earth on his feet, sinking through the dry topsoil to the coolness of the mud just below. The sound of birds high in the trees. The movement all around him. The constant wails of the monkeys. How could a man not love this? He loved the hot, humid thickness that acted as a canopy over them. Most of the surrounding terrain was mountainous, but as you got closer to the Atlantic Ocean, the mangrove swamps overtook everything.

He reached the end of the path and stood above an expansive rice field where several workers were busy preparing a new section. He watched them intently. This was also good. Work. He couldn't help but feel excited. It was planting time. The future lay before him.

He noticed Bato, his brother-in-law, making his way toward him. Bato was a short man with a big grin. Sengbe couldn't help feeling Bato's playful but growing jealousy.

"If it doesn't rain soon, I expect you to admit that I *might* know something about farming." Bato wore three short scars on both sides of his chest, the mark of the Mende.

Sengbe watched them move as he talked. "It will rain." Then Sengbe smiled.

Bato looked up. There wasn't a cloud in the sky, but Bato knew he couldn't completely discount Sengbe's prediction of rain. He knew one could never count Sengbe out. Especially when it came to the forces of nature.

"No clouds, Sengbe. How is it going to rain?"

"Bato, remember last season? Do you recall we had nearly the same conversation?"

Bato couldn't help letting a chuckle leave his body. He'd almost forgotten. "Yes. I remember. My brain is not feeble. I can remember."

Sengbe moved closer to Bato and showed his

teeth. "Then you will remember that it rained that very day."

Bato nodded.

Sengbe put his arms around Bato, "It will rain." And then he clapped Bato on the back and headed into the field.

He and the other workers labored hard that day. Sengbe now stood in nearly the same spot he had early that morning. The paddy was nearly completed. He was already looking forward to the coming celebration. The workers were slowly scattering. Bato joined him once again. They often stood there at the end of the day, taking it all in.

"We will have a good crop this year." Bato put a small stick in his mouth and began chewing furiously.

Sengbe nodded slightly. "Yes. It is all we can hope for."

"The rest of us are heading back to the village. Are you ready to leave?"

Sengbe just stood there, staring at the rice fields.

"Sengbe?"

"No, Bato, you go ahead, maybe we can have rum together tonight by the fire."

"Only if you promise to dance when it rains." Bato waved and disappeared with the other men into the brush.

Sengbe stood there for the longest time. You

place a seed, a dormant presence, under the dirt, and then you pray for rain. If it comes, you may get everything you need. You must plant with hope.

Sengbe smiled. Yes, now at twenty-five, he was at his strongest. This was indeed a time he could plant with hope. The sun was almost at rest. He began his trek back home. As he made the last turn in the path, the village just barely in sight now, he stopped and looked up. There was a mass of clouds forming almost like magic above him. There was a distant rumble of thunder. And he began to feel the raindrops—one at a time— large, explosive raindrops as they splattered on his skin. He held out a hand, palm turned up. The rains were coming. He couldn't help breaking into a large smile. He would have much fun with Bato tonight.

And then another feeling quickly replaced the lightness. It was heavy with fear and dread. It descended around him like the cover from the clouds that brought the rains that they needed so much.

Sengbe heard the breathing first. He knew there were more than one of them. They seemed to materialize out of thin air. There were three men, one of whom he immediately recognized as Birmaja. Sengbe knew then he was in trouble. It was Birmaja to whom he was indebted. He then remembered that the other two were also Vai tribesmen, named Seleh and Mayagalilo.

He knew even before he saw them that *he* was what they were after. He'd known people, men mostly, who had been stolen. Taken in midstride right from their paths. Disappearing into the blend of memory and horror. You never forgot someone who was taken, and yet you had to go on as if they'd never come back. And, to be honest, they never came back. If someone snatched you from your path when no one was around, you became a ghost.

He immediately began trying to run. A roughly made net, probably used in trapping animals, fluttered over his head in an instant and then settled all around him. The three men closed in on him.

Someone's arm moved quickly around his neck. Sengbe twisted quickly, hoping to throw the net off, but the more he fought, the further entwined he became. He cursed them. Called them names.

The arm was strong and choked his voice. He swung his fists in rapid swirls, occasionally feeling them connect with the bodies of his attackers. But there were too many for him to fight, and the net defeated him at every turn, though he fought with everything he had. All the energy, all the power he could bring to the moment he brought to his feet and his hands.

And then it was as though the world slowed down. His vision became hawkeye sharp. He looked at Birmaja. A debt had caused this man to treat him like an animal. Could Birmaja really be doing this?

The truth was that the village was just out of sight. But his eyes saw past what was in front of him. Sengbe felt as if he were somehow in two places at the same time. Even as his arm was being twisted and locked to his neck manacle, it was as though he was safe within the confines of the village at the same time. He could see his friends, his neighbors going about their early evening chores. He saw his wife kneeling in their yard, his daughters sitting beside her. She looked up, turning her head in his direction. He tried to call her. In between the blood that was now around his face and the flurry of activity he called to her. And he was sure she heard him. He hoped she'd heard him.

And then, Birmaja, the only one with a gun, hit Sengbe on the side of his head with the stock. All of the visions and the hopeful thoughts slowly disappeared and left only a darkness in Sengbe's head. He lost his legs and felt himself collapsing. Birmaja and Seleh stood over him a moment, then roughly stood him up and dragged him off.

In his head he was still screaming. But in fact, Sengbe half conscious and manacled was being pulled and pushed along by Birmaja and Seleh.

They traveled along the edge of the forest deep into the night. And even though they were often under the cover of trees, the men could feel the rain pounding steadily on the outstretched arms of the mahogany and cocoa trees. Before long the ground beneath them was slick and soft. Twice Birmaja had slipped and caused everyone except Mayagalilo to fall into the mud.

Eventually Mayagalilo decided they could stop to rest. By this time all of them were covered in mud. Seleh and Mayagalilo found a narrow tree, to which they tied a limp, and hungry Sengbe. Birmaja also undid the neck manacle, then thought better of it. "Better keep this on him. We can't afford for him to escape. And he's so strong."

"Strong?" Seleh sneered at Sengbe. "Look at the farmer now. I think we are stronger."

"Still, use them."

Later, Sengbe sat there and watched as they built a fire. He listened carefully, trying to put the pieces of what was happening to him together. But he could hear very little. They talked in whispers as they ate and the creeping darkness was like a blanket that settled over them. Sengbe's ears had to compete with the surrounding noises of the bush and the crackle of the smoldering fire.

He thought about his predicament. A person usually fell into slavery in one of three ways. They were either captured in war and then sold into slavery, kidnapped to pay a debt by fellow and/ or competing tribesman, or they were hunted and trapped by white slavers and their mercenaries. Sengbe knew that he was in a dire situation.

Once captured, a man could be sold for a crate of guns and ammunition and two barrels of rum, jewelry, fabric, or glasswares; or any combination of these things. There were any number of ways to pay for a slave. And it was well known that there was a Spaniard in a heavily fortified encampment at the mouth of the Galinas River who paid well and broadcast an open solicitation for the valuable human cargo.

After a while, Birmaja walked over to him. He stood there with a scowl on his face.

"Birmaja, why are you doing this to me? You know what will happen. You know I will be lost."

"I can't be concerned with your problems now, Sengbe. You are just unfortunate, that's all."

Sengbe's body ached throughout. There was one last chance that he could sway Birmaja to reconsider his action. He watched the shadows from the flames of the fire flicker on the man's dark skin and iron-cast face. "Birmaja . . ."

Birmaja's eyes narrowed. *Why beg now*, he thought? *It's too late. How pitiful the lion killer looks chained up like that.* "Do not speak to me. I'll hit you in the head again if you talk. . . ."

"I'll share the profits from my harvest with

you. I'll . . . Birmaja, I'll give you all of it, if you . . ." Sengbe's head throbbed. His legs were sore; his ribs hurt. He pleaded with his eyes, with his words. But as he looked into Birmaja's eyes, he knew his pleas were falling on fallow ground. Birmaja looked right through him. He didn't want to hear Sengbe beg. He couldn't take it. He knew what they were doing was wrong. But it was the way now, and neither Birmaja nor Sengbe could change that.

And, after only a moment of hesitation, Birmaja did what Sengbe expected him to. He slammed him in the head again. Lights like little bugs swarmed in the otherwise darkness of Sengbe's mind. He was catapulted into an emptiness, a vast swirling emptiness, in which he only felt things happen. He had no idea what they were, but things were happening.

Later that night in the darkness, just before the crease of daylight would stripe the West African sky, their party reached a small clearing where a group of seven other captives were huddled together. Guarding them were four other men, all Vai. Brothers trading brothers for trinkets, guns, and rum. It was the curse of the Western world.

Slavery had existed for generations in many tribes of Africa, but when the white man turned it into a big business, it was suddenly changed. Now the black body was a symbol of dumb, cheap labor, work animals to be imported from this rich land and distributed to those who could afford them.

Sengbe was roughly thrown into a shallow pit with the others. Above them stood the guards. But even from Sengbe's swollen eyes, it was obvious that none of these men would try to escape. They were all reduced by mistreatment to frightened stares, moans, and whimpers. He wondered how long he had been dragged along. How many hours had passed since he had gazed on his rice farm? What was his wife doing now? Did she know? Was she trying to get some of the others to hunt for him?

As he tried to focus his eyes, he caught the movement of one of the men coming toward him. Instinctively, he flinched, not knowing who or why he approached.

"Sengbe?"

Sengbe recognized the voice, but couldn't see well enough to be sure. The only thing he knew was that it was friendly. That voice belonged to someone whom he knew. It was Buakei, a nineteen-year-old man from his village. Sengbe nodded and was about to speak when one of the guards jerked him up and threaded his iron collar with a chain that connected all of the captives together. He saw Buakei ahead of him.

And then they were brusquely pulled up and onto a path, marching again, eight men in chains.

Scared. Ripped from their realities. Uncertain and yet knowing that their future would be fraught with hardship.

Buakei kept looking back. His eyes kept saying, "Help me, Sengbe. Help me." And Sengbe decided at that moment, in the rain with Buakei's pleading eyes upon him, that no matter what the struggle, he would not forsake his ancestors. He would never let go of the sweet smell of Tafe's yams or the sound of his children's laughter or the stories his father would tell. He would not live this life without hope. He could see that his enslavement depended on his willingness to keep living. Suppose he just dropped to his knees in the soil of his ancestors? Right there. Right now. Suppose he refused to make the march to Lomboko, the slave factory? What then? They would kill him, of course. But he would die in the land where he was born. In the arms of his ancestors.

As they moved on, even with an arm chained to his neck manacle, Sengbe knew he wanted to live. He could tell that Buakei wanted to live. And live they would.

The party traveled west and south. Silence was strictly enforced by the guards. As they walked, they tripped over each other's feet and dodged the hanging fronds and branches which whipped about in the strident winds of the rainy season. They now walked on mud that seemed to get deeper and deeper as they went on. Sengbe found himself time and again reaching for the charm his wife had given to him when they were married. He decided to tear the rawhide strip that held the charm around his biceps. Now he held it tightly. It was as though he could feel his family in his hands. This made him stronger.

Eventually they reached a riverbed. Sengbe figured it was the Galinas, flowing briskly for the usually flaccid river, with added rainwater.

The Galinas River and the river port of Lomboko were the centers of the West African slave trade. It was here that men, women, and children lost themselves. Had a part of themselves stripped away and replaced with another identity, an identity that wasn't as specific as even a number. They were suddenly not people at all but cattle. A herd of mules. Destined for service. Their deaths were already calculated in the opportunity costs of the slave traders.

There was a moment when everyone was just standing around. Buakei worked his way closer to Sengbe. They had never been good friends, but Buakei desperately needed to talk to someone who knew him.

"What are they going to do to us?" he asked.

"We're headed for the water. The big water. I'm afraid, Buakei, that we will disappear into another world from there." Sengbe thought he could see tears in his eyes. But he wasn't sure.

"Is there nothing we can do?" Buakei asked.

"I think, Buakei, that if we trust the power"—Sengbe paused and brought his upper arm into view—"these," he said nodding to the charms wrapped around his arm. "We have to believe that these will bring us back."

There was a tug at the chains, and they all realized that it was time to move on. The group headed along the banks of the river. They moved with the westward flow of the rush of the waters alongside them.

Less than an hour later, the sun began to paint yellow and orange ribbons across the sky. The prisoners were tired and hungry. The coming dawn had choked off the clouds and intermittent rain, with glorious colors that broke above them like flowers. But as they followed the path of the Galinas into the Bay of Lomboko, their hearts dropped. For there, at Lomboko was the famed "slave factory" or barracoons as the Spanish called them, owned by the extravagant Don Pedro Blanco.

The Lomboko slave factory was a massive structure made of thick, strong tree trunks driven deep into the ground. As they got closer and closer, Sengbe could see that the trunks had been shaved clean of their bark and were smooth, making them to easy to climb. They were lashed together with long iron rods.

Sengbe, Buakei, and the rest of men where herded through the gate of this fortlike structure. Sengbe looked above them, where he saw a contingent of guards, some African Krio who labored for the slavers in exchange for their freedom, some Spanish, and some of mixed ancestry. Most paraded over them with machetes, while many of the Spaniards were armed with muskets.

As soon as the group was through the gate, they were greeted by the eyes of hundreds of other captives being held there. One of the *barracoon* guards passed among the new arrivals, snatching charms and decorations from their bodies. Before Sengbe knew what was happening, all of the charms had been ripped from his arms. But in his hand was the one his wife had given him. He'd taken it off hours ago for this very reason. He suspected that anyone who knew the Mende would know that taking their charms was one way of trying to control them. Remove the deities of your enemies. Destroy their *gris-gris* and you destroy them. He looked down at his hand, opened it just enough to reassure himself and closed it again.

It was then that he realized how helpless he was. What could they do? There were maybe three hundred of them trapped there. Children. Men. Women. Kono. Sherbro. Fula. Mandingo. Kissi. Mende. His eyes lingered on a Muslim man praying. They were from everywhere. Each one waiting for a slaver to come and purchase them. Thousands more had passed through this *barracoon* before them. Sengbe's eyes settled on a small man, of maybe twenty-eight. They locked gazes. There was such a gleam of fierceness emanating from the little man. And then, he smiled at Sengbe and exposed a mouthful of pointed teeth. Sengbe had never seen such a thing. He turned to Buakei to see if he was looking at the same scene. But he wasn't.

Buakei was watching Birmaja and Mayagalilo as they broke from the group and walked tentatively over to Don Blanco. Now Sengbe watched them as well. The Spaniard was adorned in a flowing, spotless white linen suit. It was his trademark. Sengbe watched as Don Blanco showed them the fabric, rum, and rifles that were the payment for the eight men they'd brought in.

That is what I'm worth, thought Sengbe. And then he said aloud to Buakei, "Look at them, Buakei. Look at them. They trade us like cattle."

"I can't believe it." Buakei's eyes danced in terror. "I can't believe it."

Sengbe suddenly realized that they were talking to each other without fear of punishment. Their guards were busy watching Birmaja negotiate with Don Blanco. Besides, with so many of his countrymen and women in the *barracoons*, there was a familiar feeling and smell about the place. His spirits began to rise a little.

18
Kicked

AMISTAD

Don Blanco watched his corpulent old friend and customer approach. "Welcome Don Pablo. Welcome. How good it is to see you again." Don Blanco's gesture was larger than it had to be. The sleeves of his white linen suit flapped in the harbor breeze. But then Don Blanco's manner and style were always a little larger than life. He was fabulously wealthy. Powerful. He, as much as anyone, had realized the opportunities in the slave trade and had devoted his life to exploiting them. These were his *barracoons*. His slaves. This was his port.

And, to be sure, Don Blanco was quite happy to see Don Pablo. The ships pulling into the Galinas Bay, seeking new human cargo destined for Havana, had dwindled tremendously in the early 1830s when the British, after two centuries, officially abandoned the slave trade. Some weeks it dropped to as little as a single ship leaving port loaded with African slaves. The truth was, Don Blanco was rich enough that the fluctuations of the trading of slaves barely affected him. Still, he was a businessman and he very much delighted in the making of money. Particularly the cigars and cognac that came after a successful day.

And there could be no successful day without a ship fully loaded with Africans on its way across the Atlantic. Don Blanco's barracoons were full, so each ship that made its way into the harbor was like a hungry buyer for his precious human replenishment.

It had been two days since the *Tecora* had been sighted coming into the breakwater. That had brought a twinkle to his eyes. The *Tecora* was a Portuguese deep-sea schooner built to navigate the middle passage. Don Blanco had decided to personally meet and escort his old friend to shore in his private boat.

Don Pablo nodded profusely. He was finally glad to have arrived in Galinas, if only because it meant that his journey was half complete. He, too, was a businessman, not a seafarer. He wanted to make a quick but careful selection of slave stock, conclude negotiations with the extravagant Don Blanco, and leave. The life of a slaver was not without its worries. There were British patrol ships continuously roaming the West African coast. There were pirates, mutinies, and uprisings. And, perhaps more dangerous than all of those was the unpredictable rage of the sea.

They passed through the gates. Ahead of them, Don Blanco's workers roused the captives and lined them up as the Spaniards approached each barrack. They walked through the slave factory, feeling the grumbling, confused, angry, frightened turmoil of the new captives. Most of those held here had been at the start of this April free people. And each one of them had, through terror and intimidation, become a prisoner with a future that could only get worse.

"Here, look at this one." Don Blanco stood in front of one of the men in Sengbe's group. He instinctively reached up to the man's mouth and slipped his fingers between the lips and gums of the frightened man. "Strong. Healthy. You are getting warriors this time, Don Pablo. They make the best workers once they're broken. Very loyal."

Don Pablo was silent. Yes. He would take that one. And then they were in front of Sengbe, who was now sitting on his haunches. Don Blanco motioned for Sengbe to rise. But Sengbe remained as he was. He stared up at Don Blanco. It was the first time he had been this close to a white man, if that was what Don Blanco was. Both of the men, in their clothes and finery were more black than white.

Sengbe took a deep breath. He smelled them. It

was different from the thick smoky sweetness of Africa. He thought there was a acrid tinge hidden in their scent. He would remember that. Maybe it would be useful when he attempted his escape. He had already decided that he would at least try to get away. They were chained and the *barracoons* seemed so formidable, but if he was vigilant and thoughtful, he might find a way out.

But he would not jump up just because this ghost of a man asked him to. He sat still.

Don Blanco kicked at him. "Up. Get up so I can see you better."

Sengbe understood perfectly what was being asked of him. He was tired. He didn't like being poked at and displayed like a chicken at the market. If they wanted anything from him, they would have to force it from him.

Without warning, at the barely noticeable raised eyebrow from Don Blanco, two men were upon him, beating him with sticks. He felt each blow on his hands and arms as he tried to shield himself. He felt the welts and bruises as they flowered on his body already. He would remember each one. Each swing of the baton.

Don Blanco and Don Pablo casually strolled away. "It begins at the beginning, my dear Don Pablo. Any hesitation, any sign of any defiance must be dealt with swiftly. These are fierce, strong men and women." Now was when one had to be tough. The sea weakened everyone. The Africans were often decimated by the journey.

Don Pablo had carried enough slaves to know how to deal with them. "You run a tight operation here. Very high quality. Reliable."

"Yes. Yes, indeed. It is my jewel, if you will. Stop a moment. Take in a deep breath. Ah . . . yes. That is the smell of Africa, Don Pablo. You've been away too long." He paused. "Inhale that. That is the smell of Africa."

Don Pablo smiled and produced a cigar. "Of Africa *and* Africans, Don Blanco."

19
The Middle Passage

THE ATLANTIC

"A plant's growth depends upon its roots; cut them off and it withers."

Two days later three more ships laid anchor in the harbor. They were all there to take on their share of the human cargo. In the noonday sun, the flow of Africans was like a slurry of human material out of the fortlike structures scattered about the islands surrounding the bay. They moved in thin long lines as molten lava might into the sea. As though the rich soil of Africa were erupting people.

The waters of the Galinas Bay were suddenly jammed with canoes, each one containing five or six Africans, bound for one of the four ships. Sengbe was in one of them. Sengbe had been purchased along with Buakei and a number of other Mende men by Don Pablo. And, together, they were just a small percentage of the people who would not be people anymore, but slaves.

Sengbe looked at the ship on which he was destined to cross the Atlantic. *La Tecora* was written on its bow. Each of the small boats would slide alongside the *Tecora* and disgorge itself of its black jewels.

He was once again manacled to five others. As they pulled up to the gangway, the captives were pushed up the ladder and onto the quarterdeck where each one was turned to face a Spanish monk.

"La bendicíon de Dios, Todopoderoso Padre, hijo, y el Espiritu Santo." The monk blessed them with his words and by the sign of the cross. When it was Sengbe's turn, he recoiled just slightly— partly in fear and partly because he didn't want the shrouded figure to touch him. Instead he clutched his wife's charm tighter.

And then someone approached him and ripped off the loincloth he'd been wearing. Someone else threw a bucket of saltwater on him. Sengbe still had open wounds from the beating he'd already taken in the *barracoons* and when the water hit them, there was a painful sting that riveted his whole body.

Still Don Pablo moved closer and ran his hands over his body. Feeling his rippled thighs, his powerful arms. A hand on his jaw. Fingers forcing him to open his eyes wider.

"Very nice, eh, Captain? He will do well in the fields. Bring a very handsome price I would think." Don Pablo smiled.

"If he makes it." The red-haired American captain of the *Tecora* had seen many transatlantic journeys erase stronger men. "Some of them can't take it. The voyage is rough, as you well know, sir. Some of these Africans are like nails or iron spikes or something. You can bend them, but they don't break. They just keep going. That's what makes them such good cargo. But of course, just like in anything else, there are the weak ones. No matter how careful you are, you'll always get a group that just don't have the constitution for it."

"He's a stubborn one. I saw Don Blanco's men beat him a few days ago, back at the *barracoon*."

The captain looked closer at Sengbe. In Sengbe's eyes he saw the flickering glow of anger, of confusion. Sengbe wanted to spit on this white man with red hair, this demon who had dared to treat him like this.

Sengbe was then pushed toward the slave decks. He fought the pressure that pushed him along as long as he could. He looked out over the starboard side of the ship. There was Africa. Her lush fullness filled every open space. Sengbe felt tears rising in his eyes. He wondered if he'd ever see it again. Ever walk upon that path he'd been on when Birmaja waylaid him.

Suddenly someone shoved him forward and he was swallowed up by the dark, stale air of the slave decks.

The *Tecora* was one of the toughest in Don

Pablo's fleet. It was a two-masted seagoing schooner, fit enough to tame every storm they'd encountered. True, she had seen better days. But when its sails were full and the lines cast off—barring the worst of the unpredictable fortunes of the sea—the *Tecora* could be counted on to reach Havana.

The hours before the ship put out to sea were busy. Above decks there was the buzz of energy, the gathering of anticipation, the earnest, efficient attempt to secure the cargo, both human and not, for the three-month long, often arduous, voyage back home. There was no foolproof way to prepare for the Atlantic. Any ship, with any crew and captain could be caught unawares in the flexing muscle of the Atlantic deep. But the mark of a good captain was his ability to read the stars, the winds, the clouds, the sounds of the water, and the hearts of his crew. That was how this captain had developed his reputation. He was known to be a skipper who made decisions, even tough decisions, without hesitation. He always seemed to know what do. The *Tecora* and its crew had always come through.

Sengbe couldn't catch up with his own emotions. He was angry, tired, and sore. And although there were more than seven hundred other people all around him, he felt lonely and isolated. He knew that Buakei was near and there were others he recognized from the *barracoons*, but he had no interest at the moment in conversation.

He lifted his head and looked around. It was a depressing scene. The atmosphere below decks was very different from the one that existed above. Everywhere Sengbe looked there were black faces. Some fighting tears, trembling and sweating. Others given up completely to the terror. For most, this was their first time on a ship. And they knew they were on their way to another existence. They were all frightened.

Don Pablo had packed them in tight. They lay side by side and end to end in rows only eighteen inches wide. There was only four feet from deck to the ceiling in the slave holds so a person couldn't stand up. One had to crouch to move around. But the prisoners couldn't move anyway, because they were chained in place. Sengbe would occasionally push against the iron restraints just to test their strength.

If one removed the above decks and looked down on them, it would have looked like a series of anchovy tins. And indeed, there was a philosophy in this. There were slavers that took less cargo and treated them better, trying to diminish the losses during the long voyage. There were others, like Don Pablo and his captain, who were known for their ability to cram as many people into as small a space as possible. They expected to lose a lot of their captives, but because they started with more, they'd end up with more. At least, that was the thinking. It was a dance with the devil, regardless of the music.

Sengbe could see it, feel it all around him as the rising sound of misery began to waft about the timbers like ghosts. This was so much worse than being at the *barracoons*. There they at least had space. As he lifted his head and looked around the hold, he realized how many of his countrymen were shackled there. And while there were lots of men, for the first time, Sengbe realized that maybe half of them were women and children.

What was this madness? Why were they doing this? Where were they going? He felt his breath come faster. He pushed against the irons around his wrists and ankles.

"Who here is Mende?" he screamed. The air was already becoming thick with the sounds of heavy-breathing people.

"I am. From Kenema," came from someone on his right.

"And me, from Moyamba." Slowly, one after the other, the voices of his tribe filled the hold.

And then there was another call, this time from very near him. "I am Temne. Who here is Temne?"

And then the Temne added their voices. And next came the Kissi, of which there was one, the man who was very small in stature and who had a mouthful of teeth filed to points. And then the Mandingo, the Lorma, the Sherbro, the Fula, and the Kono, until the slave decks trembled under the cacophony of their voices. They were all speaking the same fear. The same anger. They were weaving their prayers together. Some voices were hollow and frightened. Some were enraged, railing against the people who enslaved them. There were voices that screamed unintelligible sounds and those full of tears. A lot of people were crying.

It was happening to everybody at once. Everyone, it seemed, at the same time realized that it wasn't a dream. That they were bound and chained in the belly of a ship. A ship. And that that ship was about to sail away. This was what the Middle Passage was. A long misery-filled trip to the enslavement.

Chained next to him on one side was a Temne, a substantial man named Yamba. Sengbe could feel Yamba's anger seething, emanating from his body like waves.

Yamba said to Sengbe, "We will never see our homes again. We will perish in this thing."

"Do not say that. We must keep our eyes open and look for the opportunity."

Yamba had stared at Sengbe as if he were insane, but said nothing in return.

As the *Tecora* got under way, commands from above decks swirled throughout the ship. "Fly the main mast, hoist sails, weigh anchor." The patter of the crew's feet was constant over their heads.

From deep in the hold of the ship, Sengbe could hear the anchor slowly rise as the men synchronized their efforts above deck. For the crew, raising anchor was often an exhilarating, defining moment. All unfinished business ashore would remain that way. The future lay on the other side of the horizon. But even for the experienced tar, the first hours at sea were tentative.

For the Africans, the effects were felt immediately. The first thing was the simple but disorienting effect of movement, of being adrift. This was followed by nausea for many of them. Over time, as the hours turned to days, the stifling air, the smell of vomit, feces, and urine mingled with the rhythmic rocking of the ship. It became a constant struggle to hold on to what made them human. The Africans, including those who were Mende, kept their villages spotless. They were notoriously clean, so the filth of the slave decks was an assault on all of their senses. And for those who were Mohammedans, the insult was even greater. They had lived lives which were strictly governed by religious laws. They washed before and after every meal. They prayed five times a day. From the moment they were all chained down and the ship was underway, they were bound in collective suffering.

* * *

Thirty days later, in the middle of the Atlantic, under a sharp sun and still waters, the *Tecora* had stalled. There was nearly no wind whatsoever. Its sails only fluttered in a light breeze. There was a strange quiet above decks. There was the regular clanking, like a cow bell, of the halyards as they bounced against the masts. The slosh of the small waves broke at the bow, and the occasional sounds of a dolphin, shark, or whale rising out of the deep and splattering the white crests of the Atlantic. Still, for the most part, there was a lonely silence above deck.

But below deck, it was a different story. The vast openness of the silence above was in stark contrast to the eerie, nearly supernatural atmosphere in the slave decks. Screams of pain, shouting, and weeping seemed to come out of the wood, out of the chains, and from the people. In this dark apocalyptic place, illuminated only by slivers of light from cracks in the deck above, Sengbe could just make out, among the hundreds of shadowy shapes around him, those of an ailing mother and her two young children.

Sengbe had quickly lost all track of time. In his world, things were measured by suns. It took three suns to do this or two suns to do that. But from the belly of the ship, all notion of figuring time by the presence of the sun was impossible. As time passed however, he was able to mark the increasing beatings that were taking place on the ship.

After five days out to sea, it became routine for the captain or one of the crew to snatch an African from the slave hold or pull someone out of their place during the brief periods when they were allowed on deck and beat them. For seemingly small infractions. If they hid food, drank more than their share of water, or didn't move fast enough they were beaten.

Sengbe saw one man bent over a barrel on deck and flogged mercilessly with a cat-o'-nine-tails. The sound of leather on skin was distinctive. A snapping, popping sound that made everyone flinch. And the marks the whip left were dangerous, eruptions of open flesh that oozed blood. The man suffered five strokes and his back was streaked with intricate patterns like a topologically correct map. Gashes became canyons, and scar tissue, mountain ranges. Flowing blood, rivers.

But as Sengbe watched the man being beaten, he was struck by the fact that he never once screamed or cried. He just lay there, his body jumping with every hit. When their eyes met, Sengbe nodded just slightly to show his support. But the man simply turned away.

Later Sengbe found out that the man's name was Kporna. He was also Mende and had been a blacksmith in his village. Sengbe shook his head in disbelief. The craft of the blacksmith was revered among his people and such a beating was unthinkable. But Sengbe had seen it. Each time he saw someone flogged, and he witnessed many, he swore he'd never forget the torment the victims suffered should he ever find a way to be free again.

Two weeks later, the *Tecora* was engulfed in a storm. The Africans trapped down in the slave decks were punished the hardest. Unable to brace themselves as the ship pitched, they rolled back and forth, limited only by the ever-present chains. But there was enough movement during the most tumultuous of moments of the storm that several people were thrown onto others. There was much screaming as those on the top yelled for help. The ones beneath them hollered as well that they were being crushed and smothered. There were even children at the bottom of the piles and panic all around.

Sengbe could see one woman frantically screaming at the pile of people struggling to straighten themselves out. She was trying to rescue one of her children. Sengbe recognized her as the woman he'd seen at the *barracoon* at Lomboko. He watched as she finally reached her daughter, who was already lifeless. The mother collapsed in sobs. Five died that way during the storm.

* * *

The food began to run low. And after they'd been to sea seven weeks, some of the Africans became deathly ill. There were many illnesses, and a number of people simply wasted away. Some had the bloody flux, a common malady on slave ships, as well as a variety of other dysentaries and infections.

Occasionally, when the Africans were brought on deck in small groups, they were encouraged to dance and move about. On one of those days, the water was calm and the sun provided a shimmer and there was a warm golden glow over everything. The ship's crew, who were mostly Spanish, had gathered on main deck. One of the men played a barrel organ, a contraption that looked like a giant music box, and from it emerged a kind of melodious but stiff sound. The organ player ground out a waltz as some of the rest of the crew began to dance.

This was going on as a group of Africans was allowed on deck to inhale the precious fresh air. The periods when they were allowed above were limited for fear of rebellion. As they scurried on deck in various degrees of vitality, nearby sailors, like schoolboys at some eerie cotillion, invited a few of the African women, with courteous bows and extended hands, to waltz with them.

Of course, the women had no idea of how to

waltz, or why the sailors wanted them to. Indeed the sailors didn't care about either and pressed them, leading them onto the "dance floor" and arranging their arms like those of rag dolls.

And this would have been as strange a scene as one might fear to see, were it not made even more morbid by what was happening across from them. On the port side of the main deck the remainder of the ship's crew, their faces covered by handkerchiefs, supervised the disposal of some African corpses by other slaves. They were literally being thrown overboard to the schools of sharks that now circled the *Tecora*.

Sengbe was one of those assigned to the horrendous task. He watched a corpse he had thrown overboard hit the water and sink beneath the waves. He then glanced around the deck at the weird, degrading spectacle. The dancing, the music, the bodies lying there. He then reached for the next corpse, and realized that it was a child.

He paused a moment, then threw it overboard. He heard it hit the water, to be followed immediately by the sound and fury of the swarming sharks ripping the body to shreds. It was then it struck him that the child he had thrown overboard was the one the woman had been trying to save.

Sengbe felt disgusted and completely frustrated. He was a warrior, but he was not used to this. If this was what he would have to endure, then warrior or not, he would fight to be free.

Once back in the hold, he would have conversations with Buakei and the others. Everyone wanted to do something, but no one knew what to do. The crew was armed. The Africans were chained. There seemed to be nothing they could do to change their plight.

It was obvious that the captain and Don Pedro had sacrificed food and supplies in favor of packing the ship with people, because the rations were becoming thinner and thinner. Sickness was all around them. Every morning, there were people who did not wake up. Who were hoisted from the deck and thrown overboard. And every night there were wails and prayers and chants reverberating from the timbers.

As time passed, it became increasingly necessary for a few unlucky crew members to go down in the decks to retrieve the sickest of the Africans. Sengbe would watch the ordeal with horror and growing rage. Nothing in his life had prepared him for this. He often wished that his ancestors would spirit him away. He remembered the stories he'd heard about some tribes who could fly. If he could do so, he would have.

When the Africans saw the crew enter the cramped decks, everybody fell still and silent. No one wanted to call attention to themselves. If they began coughing and could not stop, for instance, they were gathered and led above decks. And it became painfully obvious that if someone was dragged out of the hold because of sickness, there was a better chance than not that he wouldn't return. Few of the sick Africans had ever come back.

On deck, Sengbe watched as the sick were brought up from below. They were clustered together. Fifty sick Africans: men, women, and children coughing and shivering and staring blankly into the open sky. His stomach turned as he watched two boatswains thread a chain through their shackles. There was something about this action that chilled his blood. Something was about to happen. He could feel it. Some of the white crew were silent, stoic, just going about their duties. As Sengbe looked around, there was no one who would look him in the eye.

Except for another African, a woman who was amidships, bent over a tub of wash. She had a baby strapped across her chest. Sengbe realized that when he'd seen her earlier, she had had two children. He knew then that the body he'd thrown into the water had been her child's. He was on the verge of losing his stomach. There was too much misery around him. This was too painful.

He looked up to see two crewmen drag a fishing net across the deck and then lay it in front of the shackled Africans. Sengbe was suddenly conscious of how bright the sun was. He had been squinting as he peered across the deck. He had also broken a sweat, which collected on his brow and then slithered down into his eyes. He stared at the net and the men who had brought it there. What were they doing?

They returned with cannon balls, which they gently placed onto the net. Sengbe looked back to the washer woman as if to ask, "What is this? What are they doing?"

She looked at him, held his gaze for the briefest of moments. Sengbe couldn't help feeling forlorn. He was bewildered by their fate. His mind was a jumble of thoughts and screams. The chains around his ankles and his wrists were so heavy. Why did they not blindfold him as well? Then he wouldn't have to see the faces of his people so stricken with fear. This was what he thought as he saw the woman avert her eyes and slowly rise out of her crouch. She still clutched in her hands a shirt, which dripped water as she stood up. There was so much confusion about the deck; only Sengbe seemed to see her.

She stood and looked again at him. And then he saw it in her eyes. The moment he saw it, he knew what she was about to do. And there was nothing he could to do stop her. And he wanted to. He wanted to tell her that if she held on to the remnants of hope, things would turn out okay.

He wanted to tell her that their ancestors would not abandon them. They would be saved. But he could not run to her, for he was held down by chains. Nor could he say to her in the words of her language anything that might change her mind.

He watched her slowly walk to the starboard railing and in a smooth, committed movement launch herself and her baby into the raging sea. Sengbe watched her body disappear under the ship.

In his mind there was a scream, a loud piercing wail. But he quickly realized that neither he nor she had actually made a sound. He was just staring at the empty space where the woman and her baby had been standing. This was madness.

And then he was pushed again, this time back toward the hatch that led down to the slave decks. It was true: Nobody had seen them go over. The promise and the respite that death offered had embraced them both, like an extra blanket when the chill causes a shiver.

But there was a new commotion. Sengbe turned back to see that nearly every one of the forty crewmen stood on deck, eyes turned to the line of slaves being stuffed back into the hold. They carried whips. What new torture was this? And then Sengbe watched as the boatswain walked over to the group of sick people. Three of them had already fallen to the deck. It was a horrible sight. He saw many whom he knew. Some he had nodded to or even tried to speak to since his capture.

And again, the world slowed down. He turned to see the line of Africans being roughly shoved down to the slave deck. He was fast approaching the hatchway where two swarthy guards kept the line moving. But nearly everyone had stopped and was looking at the group of slumping blackness. The moans and cries that came from it made Sengbe's heart seize. This was too much sadness to fit into even a body as strong as his.

The boatswain now took the lead of chain from the first of those fifty shackled together and tied it to the net. Now everyone, everyone could guess what was happening. Sengbe turned to go toward them, but the momentum of the slaves tumbling back into the hold, the pull of the chains worked against him. And then he saw the boatswain kick the net containing the cannon balls into the water. Sengbe watched the people as they slid to the edge and flipped over, momentarily airborne. And then in a crash of water and screaming human terror, he heard them meet their ancestors.

There was now wholesale panic, above and below decks. The Africans were convinced there was no hope, no way to overcome this magic. Sengbe was dragged with the others quickly below deck and shackled into his space. He trembled in anger. He saw Fala's eyes sparkling with fury not far away. Buakei was shaking. From across the hold, Sengbe heard Yamba cursing. Were it not for the iron chains which held them, they would have exploded out of those decks.

He thought, *You'd better chain me down or kill me. Otherwise I'll fly away.* All that night he thought about birds. He wanted to be a bird. He wanted to fly.

But when he slept—which he longed for because he hoped it would blot out the image of all those people struggling in vain against the sharks—he knew that their spirits were trapped down there. They would be waiting there on the bottom of the ocean for an eternity, along with every other African who had claimed the Atlantic Ocean as a grave.

The rest of the Middle Passage was not in fact the middle of anything. It was the end. It was the end of life. There was nothing on the other side of home.

Fifteen days later, from the main topmast, a lookout shouted, "Land-ho."

There, in the distance, an island loomed. The *Tecora* had finally crossed the Atlantic and was approaching the warm Cuban waters of the Caribbean. One could smell land in the air.

"Prepare to drop anchor," called the first mate. The prospect of bringing the ship safely to anchor

and touching land raised the spirits of all the free
and nearly free souls on the ship. (For in truth,
the sailors lived wretched lives themselves.)

And then the anchor, with its large chain links
skipping on the lip of the starboard bulwark, was
slowly dropped with a crash into the water. It
was a sound that caused every seagoing swab to
stop a moment and thank whatever god they
worshipped that they'd made it through another
voyage. From the helm to the bottom of the slave
decks, it was known that they had finally reached
their destination.

"I'm not going to be an animal for them,"
Sengbe spoke out loud to no one in particular.

"It doesn't matter what you say, you will become either their animal or their food," Yamba
said without feeling.

And then someone else said in a haze of apa-
thy, "Or both."

Sengbe shuddered. He held two strong fears in
his heart. The first was that he'd never make it
home to see his family again. The second was that
this adventure would end with him being eaten
by white men. It was the one thing he feared
above all the other atrocities befalling the people
around him. He'd been beaten, starved, nearly
suffocated by the stench of the slave decks, seen
scores of his people thrown overboard along the
way. And all the time he had managed to survive.
But he would not allow anyone to eat him.

As the anchor touched the bottom and the ship gently slowed, a stillness began to settle throughout the slave decks. What was in store for them now? Sengbe raised his head and looked around. He saw Fala try to sit up. Fala almost seemed to be smiling.

20
Havana, Cuba

Don Pablo regarded the captain with renewed interest. "So we should have no problems with the officials? Yes?"

They stood in the shadow of Fort Misericordia, a massive, well-defended trading center and slave *barracoon*. It was the base of operations of one Pedro Martinez, perhaps the last of the large-scale slavers in the Americas. His name was known in New Orleans, New York, as well as throughout the Caribbean as a reliable dealer of slaves.

"You can never tell, Don Pablo. I will make the necessary papers available. All of their origins and identities have been carefully . . . ah . . . modified. But we will most certainly need to provide them with the appropriate encouragement."

"Encouragement. Bah. They want silver."

"Indeed, they do."

"And, I suppose you must give it to them?"

"Don Pablo, it is the way things are done here. You know that better than I do." The captain paused. "I think it is more difficult because as captain I'm the one who must actually make this transaction." He paused again and then, as an afterthought, said, "I think you don't like an American spending your money."

Don Pablo stared at his captain for a moment and laughed. "You Americans. You think I care only about the money? Well, to an extent you are quite right. I am a businessman. But they depend on me to get the Africans over here. Then they make me pay through the nose just to bring them ashore. I am a man of obligation, señor. Of honor." He paused with an air of grandeur. "The money is not important."

The captain smiled in return and said softly, "Then I will, with dispatch, conduct this business to your advantage. For the honor."

Don Pablo nodded and turned back in the direction of his boat. He was already thinking about finally getting into his own bed.

The captain approached the Cuban officials who sat at a small table facing the embarkation point. The baby waves of the Caribbean nibbled at the sandy shore behind them. "Good day, señors. I am the captain of the *Tecora*, a ship of Portuguese license. At your service." He bowed, and upon straightening himself, produced a sheaf of papers. "Here are the required documents."

"Please be seated, Captain. We will want to take a careful look at these."

The captain realized he was in for an intense round of negotiations. "I'm prepared, sir, to see if I can shorten these procedures." He produced one of the three pouches of silver and sat it on the table.

Instantly, everyone was bright with smiles and a joke was told. They drank coffee and talked about the voyage. Soon the Africans were roused from their decks and brought to the main deck where they were chained five or six together, loaded once again into small boats, and taken from the *Tecora*. The boats transported them the short distance from the anchorage to land.

As the men exchanged money and approvals, the slaves now began to file past them, the survivors of the floating hell. These Africans were already inhumanly strong to have lived to breathe Cuban air. But there they were. Sengbe and Yamba and Fala and Buakei and four hundred and fifty others were forced to walk down a dirt road toward the entrance to the fort.

The sun sat high upon them as they turned and passed through the massive gates to the fort. Sengbe walked shakily beside an equally unsteady Yamba. They squinted in the bright light of day. Their eyes met from time to time. And without speaking they both told the other how amazed they were. They were so far from home.

Inside the walls of this fortress the slaves were surprised with the attention they received. There were dark-skinned people moving among the Africans with bowls of rice, beans, water, and bananas.

You could have as much as you wanted of everything. From virtual starvation and sickness to this overflowing abundance of food and healing? Sengbe couldn't help but think for a second they might just be fattening them for slaughter.

Sengbe stood, staring into the mass of bodies moving around him. There were more than a thousand black people there. Many women and children. Warriors. Maimed. Sick. Frightened. All emotions and all kinds of people. There was probably every tribe of West Africa represented there. And Sengbe could see that the common members of tribes huddled together. Even here in a new world. Far away from their homeland, the ancestors called each tribe to make its home wherever they were. He watched Yamba gather the Temne into a small group.

When he looked up, he could see that there were levels to the fort. Above them, seated as in a restaurant, were groups of Spanish and Americans, who obviously found them appropriate "luncheon" entertainment.

There were two Spaniards, José Ruiz and Pedro Montes, who sat with Don Pablo and the captain of the *Tecora*. Also there, at the lip of the shoreline was a bevy of insurance agents and accountants. They talked of Africans and money over a small wooden table covered with papers.

Ruiz and Montes had been supplying various plantations with slaves for years, even though Ruiz was only twenty-four-years old. Ruiz paid $450 each for forty-nine adult males, of which Sengbe was one. Montes, in a separate transaction bought four young females, three of them girls.

Sengbe was eating a bowl of rice with Buakei when they were both snatched up and led to the *barracoon* gates. Chained to others and marched out, they were being herded to the loading dock. They followed a path that was like a parade of horrors. They walked past black people—slaves—working the cane fields with white overseers on horses towering over them. They saw the kind of wretched life that would be theirs very soon.

And then Sengbe saw one of the ghastliest things he'd ever seen, even after the Middle Passage. There along the side of the road on which they marched were lifeless black bodies tied by their thumbs to the trees they passed. His insides rose. He held his nausea back, but there was no mistaking the message. In this world he was less valuable than an animal. It was also clear that these white people were both very powerful and very cruel.

Sengbe and the other Africans were delivered by longboat onto a schooner. As they were led into this ship, Sengbe could see some of the other cargo being laid in. Bolts of linen, hardware, parasols, saddles, olive oil, calf skins, sewing needles, ladies' hose, and of particular interest were the bundles of cane knives he saw being loaded.

As he stumbled up the gangway, halfway up the side of the ship, he heard two Spanish men say something to each of the boarding Africans. The line moved slowly. It gave him a chance to survey the ship. It was smaller than the *Tecora*, though it was also a two-masted schooner. And it was black, a dull deep black which had melded with the wood. In a fog, a ship this color could virtually disappear. He saw the name painted on a lifeboat, *La Amistad*.

When it was his turn he was pulled forward.

"This one is Cinque. Joseph Cinque."

Ruiz looked at him. "Cinque." And from that moment Sengbe became Cinque.

"Ah . . . , I hope we can think of enough names."

Montes turned to him and said, "How many Juans have we used? Juan, ah . . . Nando . . . ah . . . Francisco . . . Trinidad, . . . You could help, you know."

"There will be plenty of fine Spanish names for

our precious cargo." Ruiz smiled a broad self-satisfied smile. "Don't you worry. The cemetery is full of names."

But the concern over names was an important one. There was a Spanish law passed in June of 1839 that made it illegal for slaves to be imported into Cuba. The slavers had figured a rather clever way of getting around it. There were three types of slaves in Cuba. First, there were those born within Spanish jurisdiction called Creoles. Next, there were the Ladinos who had been inhabitants on the island for a long period of time. And lastly, there were the Bozales who were slaves that had been imported recently from Africa. But when people bought Bozales, of which these Africans would have been, they just had to change their names and make records that said they were either Ladinos or Creoles, thus getting around the law.

And then, as had been true nearly every day since his capture—just when he would have naturally wanted to sit down and open his arms to the warmth of the sun or watch the sleekness of the Caribbean roll out from the shore like liquid glass—someone began tugging at his chains, pulling him in a different direction. Sometimes he just wanted to dawdle. To decide for himself when it was time to disappear into the casket-sized cubby that he was forced to live in.

Cinque found himself behind Fala as they were

being marched across the deck. He watched the little Kissi staring at another young man, who stood just ahead of them. The young man was Celestino, a Creole and the cook of the *Amistad*.

As the others began to move toward the ladder which would lead them into the bowels of the small black ship, Cinque now saw Celestino chopping away on a slab of salted beef. Fala was still staring at him as well. As they watched the man bring the cleaver down on the meat, Cinque could see his expression change. It was like he almost laughed with each swing of the cleaver. But as he worked it out of the chopping block, he grimaced and seemed on the verge of tears. And then, just as the cleaver was freed from the block, the man looked up to see that Fala was staring at him.

He looked deep into Fala's eyes. Beyond his eyes, into his soul and he could see precisely what they were all was afraid of. Their worst fear. Cruelty was obviously contagious because this man who did not know Fala, who was more like Fala than Montes and Ruiz or even the captain of the *Amistad*, looked now at the cleaver and pointed with his brown finger at the blade. When Cinque looked back at his eyes, he saw only the sinister smile. He knew that Fala saw the same thing.

They passed right in front of the cook. And

then, just as they reached the hold, Fala intensified his glare. It was a silent threat.

Cinque also stopped and opened his eyes to the sunlight one last time. But as he looked around, the stain of slavery and its movements disturbed whatever beauty Havana had. He saw the line of Africans being driven up the gangplanks of a number of other ships in the harbor. He saw fierce partings, people being torn apart, sold to separate slavers. Mothers and children being ripped from each other. Lovers. It didn't matter.

There was no mercy. No thought rose above the system of seeing the slaves now as animals, as less than human. Give them new names. Teach them a new language if they need a language at all. There were no mothers among slaves at the *barracoons*. No husbands. No children. No wives.

Then finally, he could see back on shore, on the road that led from the fort to the shoreline, the bodies of African men swinging in the reluctant Caribbean breeze from a massive gallows that lined the road.

And why were they there? What had they done to win their freedom? That was his last thought before being entombed again, on yet another slave ship. Someone shoved him into a space, two feet in width, with just four feet from deck to ceiling. No better, indeed, and perhaps worse than the *Tecora*'s quarters.

For the first time since he'd left Africa his mind

felt sharp again. Perhaps it was the time he'd spent in the fresh air. Maybe it was the growing feeling in him that nothing and no one was going to rescue him. Maybe he had finally relinquished the notion that the spirits would not forget him. He had certainly been forgotten. As had everyone taken from his homeland. They were all adrift without the benefit of their ancestors.

It was hard, after you have lived twenty-five years in absolute freedom, to believe that someone could exact such misery and suffering on you without any apparent consequences.

Cinque and Yamba, chained together during much of their time aboard ship, had developed a sort of uneasy, competitive relationship. Among the Africans, Cinque had been the most vocal about trying to escape and he was considerably larger than most of the other men. Yamba didn't like to admit it, but that angered him a little. Cinque often acted as if he was above the influence of Yamba who felt, as a Temne, he was the natural leader.

But when the time came to throw off the chains and storm the deck of the Amistad, it was Cinque who had willed them forward. He who had killed the captain and he who had wanted to kill Ruiz and Montes.

That was his story. From beginning to New Haven.

21
Give Us Free

The story unfolded like a dream as Cinque told it again on the witness stand, with Covey translating to a courtroom of rapt, even stunned people. The gallery was filled. They'd even had to bring in extra chairs. Curiously, a large number of blacks were present.

In Cinque's pocket was the charm and the spirit of his family. In his chest was a growing sense of clarity and in his mouth was the truth as he felt it.

"I wanted to kill them, too," he said about Ruiz and Montes. "But they convinced some of us that they would take us back home." Covey translated.

"Thank you, sir." Baldwin brought his testimony to a close.

The new judge, Bertrand Coglin, looked down at all of the principals: Cinque, Baldwin, Covey, and William Holabird. "Mr. Prosecutor?"

Holabird took a step toward the defense table. "Quite a tale. Intrigue, abduction, courage in the face of unspeakable suffering . . . and all true." Cinque nodded. Holabird stared at him a second and then nodded himself. It wasn't a friendly nod nor one that held any support. His was meant as a threat.

"All right, tell me if this is true: certain tribes in Africa, for hundreds of years—thousands, perhaps—have owned slaves."

"Yes," Cinque answered through Covey.

"Under what circumstances might one end up a slave, say among the Mende, of which you claim to belong?"

"Wars . . . ah . . . debts."

Baldwin became just a little nervous. He wasn't sure exactly where Holabird was taking this.

"I see. And how many men are indebted to you?"

"Your Honor—" Baldwin was up with an objection.

And Covey suddenly rose above his role as translator with, "I don't think you do see."

District Attorney Holabird turned to Covey and said, "Who asked you?"

"It's different," Covey said.

"Who asked you?" Holabird repeated.

Judge Coglin turned his attention to the black translator. Covey had no standing in his courtroom. "Ensign Covey—"

"Your Honor, the Mende word for slave, in fact is 'worker' because that is closer to the meaning."

Holabird jumped in. "Do these workers own the land they work on? Do they receive wages? Are they free to not work if they so choose?"

"Your Honor, now he's questioning the translator," Baldwin said in an indignant tone.

"The translator is answering for the witness," Holabird said.

But Baldwin sought to curb Holabird. "The witness is not being given a chance to answer."

Holabird would not back down. "Fine, Mr. Baldwin. Slavery, indentured servitude, whatever they want to call it. I don't care. The concept is the same. He is familiar with the concept." Holabird pointed to Cinque. "And when you get right down to it, it's all about money, isn't it? Slaves, production, money. That's the idea of it. Whether it's here or there. But I'm confused. Do your people routinely slaughter their slaves in the manner you so vividly described to us?"

Covey was furiously trying to keep up with Holabird. But the district attorney continued his pace. "Of course not. What's the point of that? Killing your own slaves is rather like burning down your own house, or hut, isn't it? How do you explain this paradox?"

Only Covey's voice was heard then as he finished his translation. The thick, sweet-sounding Mende was like music. Cinque looked up at Holabird, bewildered again. "I don't understand what you mean."

"Sure you do. As does everyone here. The behavior you attribute to your tormentors, your victims to be more precise, and therefore every other aspect of your testimony, makes no sense. Not even to you. But thank you for it. Like all good works of fiction, it was entertaining." He turned on a dime and ended with, "Nothing more."

The judge dismissed Cinque. Baldwin then called Captain Fitzgerald, Covey's superior, to the stand. His strategy involved the expert testimony of the captain. He would have to take it slow, but his goal was to prove that Cinque and the others were victims of slave traders. "Captain Fitzgerald, please explain to us your primary duties in Her Majesty's Navy."

"To patrol the Ivory Coast for slave ships." Captain Fitzgerald's voice was deep and resonant.

"Because . . . ?"

"Because slavery is banned by British law, sir."

"Yet," Baldwin began, "the abduction of freemen from the British Protectorate of Sierra Leone and their illegal transportation to the New World as described by Cinque is not unheard of, is it?"

The captain thought for a moment. "Not even unusual, regrettably."

"What, if anything in his account of his ordeal do you find believable?" Baldwin wanted the court to realize that irrespective of the laws against slave trading, it continued unabated.

"His description of the slave factory for one thing. There is such a place."

Baldwin seemed satisfied with his answer and brought his questioning to an end.

John Forsyth had drawn this straw. He had decided to argue this aspect of the state's case. He stood up. "You've seen it?"

"No, sir, we've not been able to locate it. But there is overwhelming evidence that it's real."

"What evidence, exactly? Rumor?" Forsyth wanted to make the point that there still was no concrete proof of continuing slave trade from West Africa.

"Reports."

"By reports you mean of the variety Cinque shared with us today?" Forsyth continued the tact of trying to show that the stories of slave trading were greatly exaggerated.

"It's existence, sir, has been reported," Fitzgerald repeated.

"The existence of gold mines in the Far West has been 'reported,' Captain. But I'm not about to rush out there with a panning tin. Are you?"

In cross-examination, Baldwin reapproached Fitzgerald. "Cinque describes the cold-blooded murder of a significant portion of the people on board the *Tecora*. Mr. Holabird sees this as a paradox. Do you, sir?"

The captain shifted position in the witness box. "Often when slavers are intercepted or believe they might be, they simply throw all the prisoners overboard and thereby rid themselves of the evidence of their crime."

"Drown hundreds of people?" Baldwin wanted everyone to realize the horror.

"Yes."

And then Holabird was up defending his earlier points. "This hardly seems a lucrative business to me. This slave trading. Going to all that trouble rounding everybody up only to throw them overboard."

Fitzgerald understood his point, but it was clear that the district attorney didn't fully comprehend the financial benefits. It didn't matter how many slaves were lost at any particular moment. Over the long haul, it was very profitable. "No. It's very lucrative."

After Holabird was finished, Baldwin was up again. Now was the time. "If only we could corroborate Cinque's story somehow. With evidence of some kind."

"The inventory," Fitzgerald said absently.

Baldwin looked surprised, but had planned this move all the while. He held up the same papers he'd held up when Judson was the judge. "This? From the *Tecora*?"

"If you look, there's a notation. Made on May

10th, correcting the number of slaves on board. Reducing their number by fifty."

"What does that mean?" Baldwin asked the captain.

"Well, if you look at it in conjunction with Cinque's testimony, I'd say it means this: The crew, having greatly underestimated the provisions required for the journey, solved the problem by throwing fifty people overboard."

Holabird was incensed. He jumped up and asked for the papers. They were read into the record as exhibits and then handed to him. After he quickly read them, he addressed the captain, "I'm looking at the same inventory, Captain. And I'm sorry. I don't see where it says, 'This morning we threw fifty slaves overboard.' On May 10th or any other day."

"As of course you wouldn't." The captain found Holabird distasteful. He thought the whole way in which the victims were being persecuted was distasteful.

Undeterred, Holabird pressed on. "I see that the cargo weight changed. They reduced some poundage I see. But that is all."

"It's simple," answered Fitzgerald, "ghastly arithmetic."

"For you maybe. I may require a quill and parchment and a better imagination."

"What 'poundage' might you imagine the entry refers to, sir? A mast and sails perhaps?"

Cinque had been sitting quietly throughout the long convoluted discussion. When they had first started coming to court, Cinque had assumed that whatever they were going to do to them would happen much more quickly. But now, after weeks and weeks of delays and switched judges, endless talking, his patience was at an end. What were they fighting about? Whether he was a free man or not? What was a man who was not free? What was that and where did it exist except in the hull of a dark, creaking ship with iron chains clanking all around you. *People are born free*, he thought. *We are all free unless someone has the power to put you in bondage.*

He thought about trying to escape, but he was still in chains; even here in this big house with these big white men. He no longer cared what they were saying. He couldn't understand what they were saying anyway. Even with a translator, it was confusing. The way they talked. Sideways. Not straight ahead. And when he realized that, he suddenly began thinking about what he wanted most of all.

After all the talking and the haggling and the praying and fighting. He wanted to go home. To be free to go home. "Give us free."

Cinque heard the words stumble out of his mouth. He had spoken English for the first time. It had just come up that way. It had started deep inside and erupted from his mouth just that way.

He saw the people around him, the other Africans, Baldwin, Joadson, Covey, Coglin, Forsyth, and everyone else in a moment of frozen amazement.

Holabird was the first to recover. "Your Honor, please instruct the defendant that he cannot disrupt these proceedings with such outbursts. . . ."

When Cinque saw the reaction to his voice, he said again, "Give us free."

"Your Honor, if we are to have any semblance of order in this court, he must be made to understand . . ."

"Give us free." That was what he wanted. To go home.

". . . that he cannot keep screaming 'Give us free!' or anything else while I am trying to question this witness."

"Give us free." Cinque slipped into a place in which he spoke through time and space. He was in Africa, on the *Tecora*, on the *Amistad*, in the water, in jail, in chains, holding his daughter, killing the white crewman—he was everywhere. His language, his desires existed in the same full-fledged way as those of any other man. He simply wanted what had been his. "Give us free."

22
Brought to Bear

Word of the successes and maneuverings of the defendants began to ripple out and away from the New Haven court. At President Van Buren's Long Island mansion, where a small party was in progress, the case seemed to be on everyone's mind. This was particularly true of Angel Calderon de la Barca, the emissary from Spain, who was becoming increasingly insistent on the behalf of his country that the *Amistad* captives and the ship be returned to Cuba.

Van Buren had taken a brief holiday from the campaign trail and had decided to host a dinner party for a select group of political friends and supporters. Calderon's presence there was strategic, as were some of the others.

Black people moved all around them. Some took hats and announced arrivals. Some opened doors. Some cooked. And some, like the elderly black man who moved near the president, served food. A string quartet played softly in the background.

"What's most bewildering to Her Majesty"—Calderon had been ordered by his queen to press more forcefully for an end to all the delays. He had finally managed to get Van Buren in a position where he could make his case once again—"is this arrogant independence of the American courts. After all, if you cannot rule the courts, you cannot rule."

The president looked at him with a rather solemn gaze. "Señor Calderon, as any true American will tell you, it's the independence of our courts that keeps us free."

The Spaniard stiffened and became silent. He had made the wishes of his queen known. He'd pestered both the secretary of state and the president to expedite the *Amistad* matter. All to no avail.

Calderon was considering his next move when Senator John Calhoun was announced. Nearly everyone turned to the door to watch the imposing man relinquish his overcoat to the butler. Calhoun, who had once been John Quincy Adams's vice president, had returned to congress as a senator from South Carolina.

"Thank you," Calhoun said graciously to the black man who took his coat. "I think I can navigate my way from here."

No one was more surprised than Van Buren that Calhoun had come. The president had been assured by his personal secretary, Hammond, that Calhoun would not attend. This had relieved Van Buren greatly because he knew that Calhoun, always the champion of the south and increasingly of slavery, would complicate things.

Calhoun believed that blacks were naturally inferior to whites and that white people could exist peacefully and constructively with them only as slaves. To him, concepts such as liberty and equality applied only to whites.

He was increasingly less and less apologetic about slavery. And was known to believe "mysterious Providence" had placed Negroes in a position subservient to that of the whites in the American South. And it was Calhoun, among others, who brought the demand for states' rights into vogue.

"John." The president rose to his feet with his arms extended. "I was afraid you weren't going to be able to join us."

Calhoun didn't break his countenance. He was not known to do much smiling. "You may put your fears to rest, Mr. President."

It wasn't long before the entire table was alive with discussion about the *Amistad.* The servants were busy placing food in front of each guest as Calhoun now addressed Calderon. "You see, Señor Calderon, there's a growing number of people in this part of the country who regard us in the South as not only geographically beneath them." His voice was just loud enough for everyone, particularly Van Buren, to hear.

Calhoun continued. "They ignore the fact that slavery is so interwoven into the fabric of this society that to destroy it would be to destroy us as a people. 'It's immoral,'—that's all they know. Therefore, so are we. Immoral and inferior." Calhoun smiled at the woman who placed a spoonful of peas on his plate. "We are inferior in one area. We're not as proficient in the art of profit. We're not as wealthy as our Northern neighbors. We're still struggling. Take away our life's blood now, and well, what happens then is clear to all of us. North and South: They become the masters and we the slaves. But not without a fight." He ended by infusing his last sentence with the lightness of a serious threat.

Van Buren watched as Calhoun began to taste his food. "Senator Calhoun is being modest. He's not inferior in another area: the art of exaggeration."

Calhoun completely ignored the comment and spoke again. "Now ask yourself, Señor Calderon, what court wants to be responsible for the spark that ignites the fire storm? What president wants to be in office when it comes crashing down around him?"

The senator cut into his steak. He could feel

everyone staring at him. There were no other conversations going now. "Certainly no court before this one. Certainly no president before this one." Calhoun allowed the briefest glance to Van Buren before readdressing Calderon. "So judge us not too harshly, sir. And beg Her Majesty alike. Because the real determination our courts and our president must make is not whether this ragtag group of Africans raised swords against their enemies, but rather must we?"

The message to Van Buren couldn't have been more clear. Calhoun represented perhaps the most important block of support and if Van Buren wasn't more aggressive in trying to get the Africans convicted, Calhoun would use it against him. He would try to make it seem as though Van Buren wasn't a strong friend of the slave states.

Van Buren didn't care that much about the slavery issue to risk his reelection. So, only days after that dinner, assuming that Judge Coglin would see the wisdom of the prosecutor's arguments and convict them of murder and mutiny, the president made arrangements to return the slaves to Spanish authorities.

Fully two weeks before the verdict was expected, he ordered the presence of a ship in the New Haven harbor for the purpose of transporting the Africans. The U.S.S. *Grampus*, under the command of Lieutenant John Paine, was ordered upon the delivery of the verdict to take them immediately to Cuba.

At the prison, Cinque watched Yamba leafing through his Bible. "You don't have to pretend to be interested in that. Nobody's watching but me." The air was now cold enough for it to carry words in a cloud.

Yamba looked up from the picture in his Bible to Cinque. Across the courtyard he could see Buakei talking with Maseray between the bars. But there didn't appear to be anyone else awake so early in the morning. "I'm not pretending. I'm beginning to understand it. Their people have suffered more than ours. Their lives were nothing but suffering."

Cinque listened, but was more than unconvinced. Suffered more? How was suffering measured? Compared to what? Cinque walked over to him and sat down. He wanted to see what had held Yamba's attention so strongly over the time they'd been in the prison. Yamba thumbed through the illustrated Bible. It was designed to do what it was doing: initiate those who were completely unfamiliar with Christianity. There were pictures of war and violence, of wantonness and riot. And then there was the birth of Christ.

Yamba stopped at that picture. "Then he was born and everything changed."

"Who is he?" Cinque asked.

"I don't know, but everywhere he goes he's followed by the sun. Here he is healing people with his hands. And here protecting them. And here being given children."

Cinque looked at the pictures and then at Yamba. He felt his quiet adversary had perhaps changed more than any of them. "What's this?" he asked and pointed to a picture of Christ walking on water.

"He could also walk across the sea."

Cinque looked at the picture again and had to admit to himself that the idea of walking on water was indeed an unbelievable feat.

"But then something happened. He was captured. Accused of some crime. I'm not sure what. Maybe nothing. Here he is with his hands tied."

"He must have done something."

"Why? What did we do?" He paused and Cinque was silent. Yamba continued. "Whatever it was, it was serious enough to kill him for it. Do you want to see how they killed him? You've never seen anything like this." He flipped ahead to a picture of Christ and the thieves nailed to crosses.

Cinque looked at the picture and thought then that the whole thing must have been a fabrication. "This is just a story, Yamba."

"Look. That's not the end of it. His people took his body from this thing." He moved to a new section of pictures. He made a sign of the cross in the

250

air. "They took him to a cave. They wrapped him in a cloth, just like we do. They thought he was dead, but he appeared before his people again. He spoke to them. Then finally, he rose into the sky. This is where the soul goes when you die here."

He looked around sadly. "This is where we're going when they kill us."

Cinque looked down to see the picture of Christ in heaven with his arms opened wide, beckoning. Welcoming.

"It doesn't look so bad," Yamba said with a grave softness in his voice.

Cinque was quite speechless. He regarded Yamba with new interest. How had the Temne come to believe this?

Under orders from the president, Lieutenant Paine, commanding officer of the warship *Grampus*, was under way and en route to New Haven to transport the prisoners to Cuba once they were found guilty by Judge Bertrand Coglin.

But no one really knew the mind of Coglin. When Secretary of State Forsyth put forth Coglin's name to replace Judge Judson, he had mentioned that Coglin was a Catholic. And even though he kept it as private as he could, Judge Coglin was not ashamed. He knew that many Americans still did not trust Catholics and that the bias against them was quite sharp.

And this softened his ideas about slavery. Yes,

he knew why he'd been assigned to this case. It was obvious and it was indeed a good chance to make a name for himself that might lead to a real appointment to a permanent judgeship.

But in the past few days, he'd often found himself in church, in meditation. What was the right thing to do? Could he really rule in favor of the Africans? He wasn't even sure they were human beings, much less deserving of the consideration of the court. Perhaps they truly did belong to the Spanish government, regardless of whether they would be punished for the capital crime of murder.

He'd spent a fair amount of time on his knees in prayer. He knew that not many people wanted him to ask God. They wanted him to rid the country of this challenge to slavery. And perhaps that would be his legacy.

He entered the courtroom and felt all the eyes that were fastened on him. The prosecutors Holabird, Forsyth (to whom Coglin owed his job), the defense, compact and powerful Baldwin. And of course, the defendants. Thirty-nine black faces. Some angry. Some smiling. Some indifferent. And the gallery full of more faces, white and increasing numbers of black. All wondering.

But Coglin had been aware almost from the beginning of the proceedings days ago, that Cinque held a certain power. Yes, the eyes were on the judge at the outset, but Coglin knew that soon, everyone would be watching Cinque.

"After careful review and thorough reflection . . . I find it impossible to deny the power of the government's position. There is no doubt in my mind that District Attorney Holabird, Her Catholic Majesty, Isabella of Spain, and her trusted minister, Señor Calderon have all proceeded with the utmost faith in the soundness of their case."

Cinque turned his head to Baldwin. For the first time he really tried to interpret Baldwin's face to see what was happening. And what he saw made him very uncomfortable. All the Africans were stirring. They knew this was a moment of truth. And then Baldwin closed his eyes. What could that mean?

"However, I also believe that Señors Ruiz and Montes may have misrepresented the origin of the prisoners. An issue which not only weighs crucially upon their fate, but on those of the Spaniards as well."

Cinque watched as Baldwin's eyes opened again. This time they shone with a smoldering ember of optimism. And now the prosecutors begin to shift their positions.

"Were they born in Africa? Since the answer to that fundamental question shall so heavily govern every determination of this court, I ask it again. Were they born in Africa?" And here Coglin stopped. It was more of a stop than a pause because he really wasn't sure what he was going to say. In a way he wished he could just go on stating what was true. But his job was to dispense justice.

"Yes, I believe they were." Coglin felt the hard, intimidating stare of Forsyth cut through the air. But he was also keenly aware of the energy and focus of Baldwin and Joadson and Tappan and the others there who rooted for the Africans.

"As such, Her Majesty's claims of ownership have no merit." The order in the courtroom was now dissolving. He heard loud whispers, yelps, and groans. "Neither, of course, do those for salvage made by Lieutenants Meade and Gedney. I hereby order the immediate arrest and detention of Señors Ruiz and Montes by federal marshals on the charge of slave-trading. The release of the Africans and their conveyance by this government, at her earliest convenience and expense, back to their homes in Africa."

There. He'd done it. He felt the flurry all around him and then he reached for his mallet and slammed it down. He watched Baldwin and Joadson embrace. The Africans still sat there, waiting for someone to tell them what had been decided.

"I said those men where to be arrested immediately." Coglin watched the marshals clamp the cuffs on both Ruiz and Montes. Now he was satisfied. He silently said another prayer. He knew his career was now dead in the water.

Baldwin was beside himself with joy. He found himself in Joadson's arms and loved the feel of it. They had won. He broke from his friend and said to Covey, "Tell Cinque. Tell him."

But by now Cinque had a broad smile on his face and on seeing it, Covey said, "I think he can gather."

23

The Fires of Disappointment

The celebration began in earnest as the prisoners were taken back to the stockade. They built a large bonfire of wooden planks in the courtyard. Yet the separation of the tribes continued. Each was caught up in its own interpretation of the good fortune. Each with its own chant. They all swirled together in a joyous song of different dialects.

Amidst the celebration, Buakei had pulled Cinque aside and asked him to do a great favor. Buakei needed Yamba's consent to ask Maseray to marry him. As the leader of his tribe, Yamba's approval was an absolute necessity.

Cinque sought out Yamba and found him in a group that consisted of two from his tribe, Ensign Covey, and three missionaries, one of whom was black. As Cinque approached the group, one of the missionaries spoke to him.

"God's blessing on you. We've come to teach you about the Savior, Jesus of Nazareth."

Cinque ignored the missionary and spoke in Mende to Yamba. "Come here, we have to talk about something important."

As Cinque tried to lead him away from the missionaries, Yamba resisted and said, "You should listen to them."

"I know. I will. Later."

Yamba put his hand on Cinque's shoulder. "My prayers to their God are what saved us."

"I know. Listen, my friend Buakei has asked me to talk to you about, ah . . . is her name Maseray?" Now Yamba walked with him. Cinque could feel the presence of Maseray somewhere nearby. When he looked up, he could see Buakei in the Mende camp, staring at them.

"What about her?"

"Well, he wants to marry her."

Yamba turned and walked away. Cinque hastened after him. "Yamba, she wants to marry him, too."

"I don't care. It's impossible. You know that."

The missionaries had drifted over to them, but Cinque waved them off. "Not now," he said, still in Mende.

"Your brother has accepted the Lord in his heart—"

Cinque was becoming annoyed. "I'm talking and I don't want to be interrupted."

"Your own redemption is no further—"

"I'm trying to have a conversation—"

"Our Lord, Jesus Chri—"

"Shut up!" Cinque screamed. Covey rushed over and was met by a frantic Cinque. "I can't make these people understand that I need them to be quiet. They can't seem to understand anything. Tell them." He physically turned Covey around and aimed him at the missionaries. But they kept coming at him.

"Our Lord Jesus teaches us that anything we have is yours. Our time, our love, our strength. Anything."

Covey turned back around and translated what the missionary had said for Cinque. Cinque listened and then, impetuously snatched the hat from one of their heads. He put it on his own head. Cinque then tugged at the jacket of another missionary, who initially pulled away and then relented and took off the jacket. Cinque took it and put it on. He then grabbed Yamba again and led him away.

"We need to talk about this. Those two want to marry. After all that we've been through, do you really want to keep that from happening?"

Later that night a carriage pulled up outside the prison. The clomp of the hooves on the road, the metal jangle and creak of leather were all twisted into a steady sound that broke an eerie stillness that had settled over the prison after the celebration. Baldwin, Joadson, and Tappan had road the way in silence. Perhaps the dread that was thickening around the prison came from them. Perhaps they brought it with them.

They, indeed, brought ill tidings. "This news . . . this is bad news . . . but," Tappan stuttered. Baldwin was already out of the carriage and walking through the gates of the prison. But Joadson just looked at Tappan. What was he talking about?

"The truth is, they may be more valuable to our struggle in death than in life." Tappan kept a solid expression. He was being philosophical.

But Joadson felt a rising scream of anger inside his chest.

Tappan continued. "Martyrdom, Mr. Joadson. From the dawn of Christianity, we have seen no stronger power for change. You know it's true."

"What's true, and believe me when I tell you I've seen this. There are some men whose hatred of slavery is stronger than anything, except"— Joadson tried to relax the tension in his jaw even as he completed his sentence—"except for the slave himself."

Tappan stared at him. "If your wish is to inspire such hatred in a man, Mr. Joadson, speak to him in that fashion and it may come true."

Joadson was actually glad that Tappan had spoken so clearly and forthrightly. He smiled and stepped out of the carriage. He walked around to the other side. He didn't know why this seemed the proper expression of his anger, but it was the first thing that came to him. He could have been more direct. He could have said exactly what was on his mind. He could have told Lewis Tappan that he, Theodore Joadson, was a man not a symbol. He breathed and he had a family and he got tired every day just like everyone else. Cinque and Yamba and Buakei and Maseray and all of them were people. Not just names on a ship's manifest. Not just the tokens of a movement that meant good. But people. It was so hard for some people to really understand that. Indeed the only time when you really wanted to be treated like a human being was when you weren't. You knew right away when someone was overlooking your humanity, as Joadson felt that Tappan sometimes did to the *Amistad* Africans.

Joadson walked around to the other side of the carriage and opened the door for Tappan. "Allow me to open the door for you, sir. Allow me to help you from the carriage. Careful of the mud, now." He held his hand aloft as support. But Tappan let his weight settle back into the seat. He stared ahead, insulted.

As Baldwin entered the prison he could see Cinque, Yamba, Buakei, and Maseray in some sort of a meeting. And then he saw Covey waving and coming toward him.

"A great summit is in progress," Covey said smiling.

"Well, I think you should break it up. I have to talk to Cinque."

A short time later, Baldwin, Covey, and Joadson sat across from Cinque at a table near the bonfire. Covey became the center of all conversation as the Mende flowed from Cinque into him and came out as English. And the English was transformed to Mende.

Baldwin held a heavy weight in his voice and on his face. "Our president, our 'big man' has appealed the decision to our Supreme Court." He hated saying the words.

"What does that mean?" Cinque asked.

"It means we have to try the case again."

Cinque looked at each man, wondering what was going on. Baldwin looked at him and understood his confusion.

"I know." Baldwin broke the silence. "It's hard to understand . . ."

How much was he supposed to take? When was it going to end? "No. No, you said there would be a judgment. And if we won the judgment, we'd go free."

"No, what I said—"

"No, that's what you said." Cinque's voice was strained and surging.

"No, what I . . ." Baldwin stopped even as Cin-

261

que was about to object again. He probably had said what Cinque thought he'd said. They weren't going to solve anything this way. "Okay. Maybe you're right. Maybe I did say it. I shouldn't have. What I should have said—"

Covey looked at him sadly. "I can't translate that."

"You can't translate what?" Baldwin felt exasperation growing inside him.

"Should." Covey said flatly.

Baldwin stared at Covey. "There is no word in Mende for 'should'?"

"No." Covey tried to sound calm. "You either do something or you don't."

Baldwin looked again at Cinque. "What I, ah . . . meant to say . . ." He turned his head back to Covey to get his approval.

Covey shook his head "no." "Not in the way you mean it."

Baldwin took a deep breath and began again. "What I said to you before about the judgment is almost the way it works here.

"Almost?" Cinque understood that.

Baldwin completed his thought. "But not always."

"Almost." Cinque repeated the word. Once again, Cinque felt like he was being pressed back into the slave decks. Back in a stench-ridden, tight cubbyhole that was not fit for man, woman, or beast. Was that what "almost" meant? That they would keep changing the rules until they won? And if *they* won, what would happen to him and his people?

And suddenly everything went flying. In a rage, Cinque rose from his seat and turned the table completely over. And then he was screaming, "What kind of place *is* this? Where you 'almost' mean what you say? Where laws almost work? How can you live like this?"

Covey was trying to keep up with Cinque, translating as fast as he could, but then Cinque pushed him away. He didn't need a translator anymore. He was no longer rational. Suddenly Cinque didn't want to sit at their table and discuss how much longer he'd be in chains. He looked into Baldwin's eyes and saw pure fear. It didn't matter that this white man had worked for his freedom. Now with the raging fire behind him and the raging lion inside him, he knew that Baldwin saw something to be afraid of.

This was the Cinque who had pushed his sabre into the chest of the captain of the *Amistad*. The same Cinque who avenged the death of Faloma. The same Cinque who wanted to kill Ruiz and Montes because he *knew* they meant him harm. What kind of life was this where you sat quietly while people explained your misery to you over and over again? He'd had enough.

He walked away from them and into the shadows. After a few minutes, he heard Joadson approach. He knew the sound of Joadson's boots on the dirt. He could also hear the black man's cane as it tapped lightly against the ground as he walked. But when he looked up, he saw that Joadson had also brought Covey with him. Covey now looked a little shaken. As if he wasn't completely sure what they were doing was a good thing.

Joadson spoke first. "I want to help."

Cinque held his silence. What could a black white man do? He had been in this country long enough to see that black men had no power. He'd watched all of them cleaning and cooking and polishing and washing and ironing and painting and doing all the menial tasks while white men and women strolled about the streets in oblivious splendor. Free. Even Joadson, who obviously cared and worked hard on his behalf, had no power. No one hardly ever spoke directly to him. He was just there all the time. No one seemed to value him.

"What can you do?" he said finally.

"I've never seen anyone like you, Cinque. I respect you very much. Perhaps there is another way out of here."

"Another way?"

"We've, ah, well, there's a group of folks, some colored, some white, who take a more, ah, direct approach to some of these problems." Cinque was listening now. Covey was actually trembling as he talked. He knew they were on dangerous territory.

"Maybe we can get you away from here. And then someone can get you to the next city and on until we can get you up to Canada. From there maybe you could find a way back to Africa."

Cinque nodded.

"It'll be dangerous. And I won't be able to go with you all the way. Neither will Mr. Covey. You'll pretty much be on your own."

Cinque nodded again.

"What they're doing to you is not right. There are too many political forces working against you."

"What about Baldwin?" Cinque asked.

"He can't know anything about this."

As midnight approached, it found Colonel Pendleton, the town jailer, in the Harbor Tavern with one of his guards. They were camped in a corner of the crowded and noisy pub, drinking ale. Pendleton looked up from his tankard to see Bomoseen, the crab catcher, lumber in and proceed in his direction. He nudged his companion and both of them stared at him.

Bomoseen mumbled something unintelligible and Pendleton shooed him away. "Go beg somewhere else." But Bomoseen walked right up to their table and laid a note down. He then turned away and quickly blended into the crowd.

Pendleton unfolded the paper. "Looks like we're in for a little trouble tonight. We better get going. I almost don't believe who sent this message but I'm glad he did. At any rate, he brings bad news. We've got to get to the prison right away."

They quickly left the table and headed into the chilly fall night. As soon as they were outside, Pendleton caught sight of the small man across the street, standing in the shadows. They walked in that direction. As they moved closer, it was clear that it was Baldwin standing there.

"Colonel," Baldwin said in a hushed tone, "I don't like the way this is going. There's a right way and a wrong way to do things."

"You did right, sir." was all Pendleton said as he broke into a run to rouse the volunteer militia.

Within an hour there was a buckboard wagon loaded with a contingent of militia headed to the prison.

At the prison things had changed dramatically from the time of the celebration. The three guards who were on duty had been subdued and were being held down by a group of Africans. They had taken advantage of the guards by creating a disturbance, a fake fight in one of the cells to draw all the guards into the area. Now the Africans were in possession of the muskets and the guards were facedown on the ground.

At the same time Joadson and a group of abolitionists were slowly traveling in a convoy of buckboards toward the prison. Joadson's wagon was full of supplies and rifles, things the Africans would need to make a successful escape. The other wagons would carry the Africans northward. It wasn't exactly the Underground Railroad, but Joadson hoped to make that connection along the way.

The hardest part was getting them out of New Haven. After that, it would easier. But the abolitionists were agreed on one thing: They would not engage in a confrontation with the militia. The Africans had to walk out of the prison on their own power.

Joadson pulled his wagon to a stop about a hundred yards away from the prison. The other four wagons quietly came to a stop behind him. He could see the prison gate. And there he saw Cinque in the moonlit darkness working on the gate's lock.

Earlier that evening during the bonfire, Cinque had seen numerous spikes in the planks of wood that were being used as fuel. Later, he'd rooted through the ashes and found one. Once again he used a spike to open the locks to the chains that held them down. Now he struggled with the main gate.

All of the other prisoners were gathered around him, except Yamba, who stood deep in the darkness of his cell, fondling a cross and holding his Bible as an amulet against the trouble he knew was coming.

Finally, Cinque tripped the latch of the lock and it popped open. He pulled the bolt on the wooden gates. They swung open. As a group, they all slowly, cautiously came forward.

Suddenly militiamen came into view, some dropping to a knee, their muskets aimed at the black people. Others of the militia took up position behind those kneeling.

Once outside the gate, Cinque could see the guns aimed at him, the men poised against them. He swallowed. Why did this keep happening to him? The lion. The *Amistad.* And now another moment when his life was held on the thinnest of threads. Should he press forward? How lucky was he really?

And then out of the corner of his eye, he saw the movement of a horse. A man sat on a horse. In the unreal light, he could see the guns drawn and aimed, the surging escapees, the waiting wagons in the distance. Cinque looked up at Colonel Pendleton sitting astride his horse. And beside him, also on a horse, was Roger Baldwin.

Cinque couldn't believe what he was seeing. Baldwin was the one white person he thought he could trust. But there he sat, perched on his horse, peering down at Cinque over his wire-rimmed glasses. They were locked there like that. Everyone waited for a sign from the colonel or from anyone as to what to do next. But this time, Cinque was the one to retreat. He realized instantly that his people would have been killed had they pressed forward. There was no doubt, they would have died there.

"Where did he think he was going to go? How many people was he prepared to kill?" Baldwin drank deeply from his glass. Joadson sat looking at him. "How many of his own was he prepared to have killed?"

Again Joadson didn't answer his question.

"Of course, I understand his rage. But . . ."

"Perhaps, now you're going too far." Indeed, Joadson thought, he *had* gone too far.

"I didn't say I could feel it. I said I could understand it." Baldwin looked across the table at Joadson. His smugness was beginning to irritate him. No, he wasn't black. He hadn't been enslaved. "I suppose you would have abetted him, given the chance." He thought about Joadson's visible absence during the attempted escape. "All right, why didn't you help them?"

Joadson continued staring silently.

"I suppose you think *I* should have rather than—"

Finally, Joadson cut him off. "Rather than turn him in? You're right, that is what I think. It's also what you think."

Joadson couldn't help feeling the smugness he

knew annoyed Baldwin. His family had been slaves. He was black in America. Baldwin wore his privilege like flowing robes. If he wanted to get involved, he did. If he wanted to help the Africans, he did. If he wanted to tell the police that the Africans were going to try to escape and pursue their own freedom, he did. Baldwin could do what he wanted. He was a white man in a white man's world. He could understand the rage and fight against it at the same time. He could have helped, but instead, there was something which made him defend a system that at its heart was wrong.

"Tell me, Mr. Joadson, since you obviously know me better than I know myself. Since you obviously know everything. In which should we place our trust? Laws or lawlessness?"

"When our laws apply equally to us both, Mr. Baldwin, ask me again. If you're not too drunk to do so. And I'll be happy to tell you then."

Joadson got up from the table.

But Baldwin said, "Maybe you'd prefer those in a village somewhere in Sierra Leone or wherever you're from." He was angry. He didn't mean what he was saying, but he wanted the tightly constructed Joadson to unravel. Unravel like he was doing. Everything seemed to be going wrong in a case that at first had seemed so simple. And then he had done something he hated in himself. He'd turned against Cinque. Or at least he knew that's what Cinque thought. But Baldwin really believed that if he hadn't intervened, it would have been a bloody scene when the escapees were caught. And he firmly believed they would have been caught.

But Joadson heard what he'd said and hesitated a second before walking away. That was the type of epithet he was trained to ignore. He knew that when white people were angry, black people were a safe and easy target. It was the first test of black male life. Could you ignore a derogatory remark from an angry white man without losing your composure and going after them?

Joadson also heard Baldwin scream at him as he left the pub, "I saved his life!"

24
The Meeting

"It is little drops of water that flood a river."

*To His Excellency John Quincy Adams
Massachusetts, Member, House of Representatives*

I have understood from Mr. Joadson that you
are acquainted with the plight of the Amistad
Africans. If that is true, then you are aware we
have been, at every step, successful in our presentation of their case.

Yet despite this, and despite the unlikelihood of
President Van Buren's reelection, he has appealed our most recent favorable decision to the
highest court in the land.

As I'm sure you are well aware, seven of nine
of these Supreme Court justices are themselves
Southern slave owners. This, and the clamoring
of the Imperial forces of Spain and the antidemocratic, antiabolitionist forces in our own troubled
nation present the unhappy reality of our previ-

ous victories held hollow. And the Africans, al
most certainly, threatened with death.

Sir, we need you. If ever there was a time for a
man to cast aside his daily trappings and array
himself for battle, that time has come. Cicero once
said, appealing to Claudius in defense of the Re-
public, "that the whole result of this entire war
depends on the life of one most brave and excellent man."

In our time, in this instance, I believe it depends on two: a courageous man at present in
irons in New Haven named Cinque and you, sir.

Sincerely,

Roger S. Baldwin
Attorney-at-Law

At the Pendleton's quarters, Mrs. Pendleton
was nearly ecstatic as she lined up her household
staff. They, of course, were wondering what it
was that warranted their presence in the parlor.
They quickly found out as the three young
Mende girls were ushered into the room. The
girls were outfitted in puffy white dresses with
bows and ribbons decorating their hair. They
seemed so happy that one might think that they
had been forced to be happy. But that would not
have been entirely true. The girls did like to sing
and when it came to their needs, nothing was denied them. They were Mrs. Pendleton's project.

And tonight, her project would perform their first recital. The girls began to sing and their voices were truly special, blending together in the sweetest of sounds. The audience of black folks was uncomfortable. The singing was beautiful, but where was it coming from? So, when Mrs. Pendleton said, "Isn't this wonderful?" they all smiled and nodded with no small measure of ambivalence.

Cinque could hear them singing as he paced in his cell. They'd now separated him from the others. And it made him feel more like an animal than ever before. To make matters worse, the good colonel was back to leading tour groups around the prison. Cinque could see him and a small group of people standing right above him on the catwalk.

He heard the hymn, but knew it wasn't authentic. Those girls were hiding in those beautiful voices. He thought about his wife's voice. How he'd heard her chanting for him as he lay in chains in the belly of the *Tecora* during the Middle Passage. He'd never answered her. Never sang the song back to her. Never said how much he loved her and how he'd never rest until he was back there. Suddenly he let the sound of his heart become a part of the air as he softly began to chant. Without thinking, it grew in his throat and in the night around him.

The Meeting

I pray to see my mother,
I pray to see my father,
I pray to see my children,
Back home, back home.

Buakei, who had been listening to the girls, now heard Cinque. As he listened, he realized that Cinque was trying to reach back across all the water they'd crossed and all the distance between them. Buakei's voice joined Cinque's.

And then, together their chant began to overshadow the hymn that still fluttered out of the Pendleton house. But when the girls heard the chanting, they stopped singing. Mrs. Pendleton walked to the window to see what was happening.

She was not alone in her curiosity. Joadson, at home, got up and walked to his window. He could hear them. Now, more voices than just two could be heard; it sounded as if the entire prison population had solidified into a choir. The chant was plaintive, sad, but not beaten, not a sound of hopelessness.

All along the streets bordering the prison, people were drawn to their windows by the unified chant. And even though no one except those who sang knew what they were saying, no one could deny that it was powerful. There was a force in their voices which virtually proclaimed their freedom.

* * *

John Quincy Adams was in his greenhouse when the letter came. He was in the process of repotting one of his favorites when he felt the presence of his valet standing over him. He carefully lifted the plant from its pot and laid it gently onto a potting bench. He took the letter and opened it.

When he'd finished reading it, he instinctively crumpled it up and let it fall to the ground.

It was now December and the air had turned cold. It had been snowing hard for an hour or more and James Covey was covered with snow as he came into Baldwin's office. He stamped his feet and shook the snow off as he began to remove his coat.

"Any word from—" He said to Baldwin but was cut off midsentence. He saw that Baldwin knew that he was asking whether Adams had responded or not.

"What did Cinque say?" Baldwin changed the subject.

"He won't see you." Covey moved to the fire and put hands near the flames.

"He won't see me?" Covey shook his head. "I want to talk to him. I need to see him." Baldwin was at the coatrack putting on his overcoat.

"Let's go."

Covey shook his head again. "I have to respect his wishes."

"All right. That's fine, Covey. Respect his wishes, warming your hands over somebody else's fire."

Covey expelled a long sigh, and realized that nothing had changed. They were there to help the Africans and Baldwin was still fighting. He'd signed on, too, and he wouldn't quit either. He grabbed his coat and walked out the door that Baldwin held open for him.

They rode in silence to the prison. Once there, Covey followed Baldwin through the gates and into the cell area. The guard led them to Cinque. Covey stood by the door and Baldwin ignored Cinque's gaze and sat down next to him. Cinque turned his body at an angle pointed away from Baldwin.

"Ensign Covey isn't here because he is busy respecting your wishes." Covey translated without emotion. Cinque was still and silent. "How's your English coming along?" Another silence. "No better than my Mende, I suppose."

Baldwin threw Covey a look which said, I'm not going to give up. "I realize this isn't something you necessarily want to think about. But has it occurred to you that I'm all you've got?"

Cinque continued to stare off into space.

"As it happens, since my practice has deteriorated to virtually nothing these past months, you're all *I've* got, too." He paused again. "Want to see something?" He opened his briefcase and took out a doll with pins stuck in its head. "This is I."

Cinque was listening, but didn't really have anything he wanted to say to him. Baldwin had betrayed him. He was still in prison because of him. All he had left was the charm that his wife had given him. It was almost always in his hand now.

Baldwin then removed a short length of twine, knotted into a noose. "This is *for* me." And then he took out a stack of mail. "More death threats. Some of them signed. By my own clients. I should say former clients."

Baldwin tossed everything back into his case. "That should give you some consolation, I would think. Knowing that my life has completely fallen apart." He paused again. He did feel like he was falling apart. He'd tried to ignore it, but as the days passed, that was exactly what was happening.

"There's another consequence to having no clientele to speak of, although you may not like this as much: I'm free to sit here as long as it takes for you to acknowledge me." He waited for Covey to finish the translation. "You understood that word, didn't you? Free?"

Cinque was like stone. Yes, he understood the

word. It meant freedom. It was what he didn't have and Baldwin had so much of.

"Cinque?" Baldwin asked again. And then, "We'll just sit," he said, referring to himself and Covey. Covey found a chair and dropped into it. They all sat there in silence—Cinque fondling the charm, Baldwin looking at Covey, and Covey wishing something would change.

And then a voice disturbed the stillness. "Caesar."

Baldwin turned to face the white-haired John Quincy Adams standing outside the cell.

"Cicero's appeal was to Julius Caesar, not Claudius. Claudius would not be born for another hundred years. You were right that it was one of them, though." He shrugged his shoulders. "That's not much, but it's something."

Everyone, including Baldwin was struck dumb. Cinque had no idea who the old man was at all.

"That's he?" Adams asked.

Baldwin found his voice and began to rise. "Yes, sir."

"Please unlock the door."

Baldwin learned quickly that John Quincy Adams did not take his law lightly. With only a day's notice, he was literally expected to move in with the former president. In no time it seemed that Adams had him hunting through his extensive library, retrieving obscure but obviously pertinent books.

As he walked along the balcony of the library, his arms full of books, and Adams sitting at his desk below him barking orders, Baldwin felt like he was back at law school.

"Keep going," he heard Adams call up.

"I've never heard of some of these books."

"In your prior life as real estate solicitor, Mr. Baldwin, I might imagine rather more than 'some' have not found their way into your library. There, on the second shelf, there. Fourth from the right."

Baldwin retrieved the third volume from a set of books on treaty law. He added it to the stack he was already carrying.

"Careful. Those are books, not bricks." Baldwin fairly juggled his way down the ladder.

At the prison, Covey and Cinque were talking. In his own way, Ensign Covey felt more committed to Cinque than ever. He had watched the Africans endure the interminable delays and the defeats. He'd taken to spending time teaching Cinque English and engaging the flashpot brilliance of his mind.

"The treaty is between America and Spain, yes?"

"Yes."

Cinque thought about it for a moment. "But we

were neither here nor there when we took over the ship."

"You were out at sea?"

"You see what I mean?"

"Yes." Covey was stunned. No one had asked the right question. Or even thought about it this way.

"Unless they own the sea, too, the treaty shouldn't apply."

Covey considered what Cinque was saying. That was how perceptive Cinque was. He'd made a discovery that might help his case. "I wouldn't think so."

Cinque regarded his new friend. He almost had to smile. It took an African man, a Mende, who'd been freed from slavery, but chose to join the British Navy to help him feel less like an animal. Covey could actually hear what he had to say. "Ask them about it."

Both Adams and Baldwin were immersed in their research. They were scouring every aspect of treaty and international maritime law to find a way to pry the claim of Spain from the case. There was a deep silence between and around them, disturbed only by the occasional turn of a page. Then they both heard footsteps and looked to the door at the same time. A servant stood there beside an apparently nervous Ensign James Covey.

"Yes?"

"Cinque asked me to ask you if you've thought about the question of jurisdiction?" Covey asked.

"What?" Adams had heard him well enough, but couldn't countenance the impertinence.

"That since he took over the ship at sea, and since neither Spain nor America owns the sea, how is it the treaty between . . ." Covey spewed his sentence in a breathless stream.

"No. No. Tell him, ah . . ." Adams took a deep breath. This was precious time being wasted. "Tell him that the treaty recognizes no jurisdictional limitations."

Covey stood still. He'd heard the response and was trying to distill its meaning. He saw the president go back to his work, but he remained standing there. He wanted to help Cinque and the rest of the prisoners. After all they were countrymen.

"Well?" Adams's mutton chops seemed to stand out even farther.

"He will ask me why."

"Because I said so." Covey watched as Adams waved his hand dismissively and went back to his book. But he kept his feet planted.

"I'm afraid that won't satisfy him, sir."

Adams and Baldwin were both now staring at Covey. Baldwin was actually smiling. Covey saw his smile and Adams's glower. But he stood there nonetheless.

"Tell him because both parties agreed to it.

Thus if so mutually agreed upon a contract can debar restitution by statute." Adams sighed. "Put that into Mende."

Even though he had to admit that he was a bit confused by the explanation and knew it would indeed be difficult to translate, it satisfied Covey. He could take that back to Cinque.

After he was gone, Adams looked at Baldwin, who quickly dropped his smile. Baldwin could have sworn he actually heard the former president, "harumph" as he opened a new book.

They worked through dinner. Meanwhile, Covey had traveled back to the prison and met with Cinque. And, just as he had feared, Adams's answers had actually raised another question that Cinque wanted answered. So Covey had returned.

That night the moon was full. It cast a shimmering glow which cut through the unshielded windows of the library. The light danced among the books. Covey knocked tentatively.

"Excuse me," he said as he entered. Both men watched him intently. "Cinque would like to know"—he checked his note—"that if he is the 'legal property' of Ruiz and Montes, then how does the treaty apply? Since it is between America and Spain?"

For a second Adams hesitated, following Cinque's rationale, then said, "Or their citizens. '*Or* their citizens' is included in the language. If he must know."

Once again, that satisfied Covey. He nodded to Adams, turned, and left. But before he was completely out of the door, he heard Adams say, "Good point, though."

The sun came up on Baldwin and Adams still poring through citations and briefs. They were served a breakfast of tea and pastries. But time was very short. Nothing definitive had emerged to encourage Adams that they had a strong case. He suspected that such an angle existed, he just wasn't sure that he or Baldwin would be able to come up with it before the case went to court.

And then, at the door, Covey reappeared. Adams sat back in his chair. Baldwin nearly laughed out loud. He watched as Covey unfolded a rather long piece of paper.

"Does the American government have any treaties with West Africa?" Covey said, reading almost verbatim.

"No," Adams responded. He was becoming increasingly more impressed with the way Cinque's mind worked.

"Does Spain have any treaties with West Africa?"

"No."

"Does the Commonwealth of Connecticut have any treaties with—"

The Meeting

Adams threw his hands in the air. He was impressed, but this was going nowhere. "No. No. No. Now stop this!"

Covey could see that he wasn't going to get very much more out of this exchange, so he abruptly backed out of the library and like a good messenger headed back to the man who'd sent him.

Who would have guessed that Adams would have consented, no, demanded that Cinque be allowed to visit him? Adams sensed in the urgency and the depth of thought evident in the questions Cinque was asking, a need to be intimately involved. It wasn't what he'd expected when he agreed to try the case in the highest court of the land. He knew he'd have to deal with the petulant Baldwin and perhaps even the overly sentimental Joadson, but Cinque? He was beyond shocked that Cinque had tried to interject himself in such complicated legal affairs. But as was his wont, Adams often began with a loud bark, but would slowly, almost stubbornly soften into strategic reconsideration.

He wanted to talk to Cinque. Wanted to feel the strength everyone talked about when they talked about Cinque. But more importantly, the defense he'd constructed depended on Cinque.

The next day, Cinque was brought in chains to

the library, flanked by a half dozen armed federal marshals.

"Unshackle him," Adams said tersely.

"I'm sorry, sir, I'm under strict orders to ensure the—" One of the marshals had stepped forward.

"I said, unshackle him." This was an order.

"Yes, sir, Mr. President." Adams watched the marshal fumble with the key as he began to unlock the chains.

"Now, I want you to give us leeway. Understand? I will take full responsibility." Adams shook Cinque's hand and led him toward the greenhouse. Everyone else, Baldwin, the marshals, and Covey looked at each other. Covey wondered how they were going to talk about anything without him.

Cinque had been rousted out of a sleep by Covey to tell him that he was summoned to go to meet the former president of the United States of America. He'd been chained and pushed aboard a carriage and delivered like a package. So he was a little disoriented standing there having his hand pumped up and down.

Cinque let himself be led out of the library and into the greenhouse. Adams began talking. *"Phaleonopsis,* ah, moth orchid. I brought this over from China. Yes?" he pointed to the delicate lips of the flower.

"Salix caprea, pussy willow; from France. And this is a White Monk's Hood, from England.

Blush Noisette rose from . . . well, from Washington, D.C., but don't tell anyone," he said, as he briefly touched the rose that had flowered from the plant he'd pirated from the Congressional Gardens.

Cinque understood nothing of what the old man was saying anyway. But the flowers and the greenery made him think of home. The chains were removed and he was not in prison. Altogether he was freer at this moment than any other time since he'd been kidnapped. Then Cinque noticed something very familar to him. It was an aloe plant, its succulent arms outstretched.

Adams saw Cinque's reaction and said, "Yes, African aloe. I can't tell you how difficult that was to come by."

Cinque smiled.

Adams showed him to the potting bench, a favorite place for the former president. He waved Covey in. Baldwin quietly eased himself into the greenhouse as well. But he stood well out of sight. Covey sat down and began translating.

"You understand you're going to the Supreme Court?" Cinque nodded. "Do you know why?"

Cinque answered, "It's the place where they finally kill you."

Adams smiled. "No. Well, yes, that may be true, too but it's not what I meant. There's another reason. A more important one. Although, I'll admit, perhaps more so to us than you." The ex-president realized he had lapsed into a line of discussion that made sense only to himself. "Do you know who I am? Has anyone told you about me?"

"Yes," Cinque said flatly.

"What have they told you?"

"You are a chief."

"Was a chief."

"A chief can't become anything less than a chief," Cinque responded instinctively. "Even in death."

It was Adams's turn to smile. "Oh how I wish such were true here, Cinque. You've no idea." He paused and could see in Cinque's eyes a measure of confusion. "One tries to govern wisely, strongly. One tries to govern in a way that betters the lives of one's villagers. One tries to kill the lion."

When Cinque heard the reference to the lion, he was struck by how history followed people like shadows.

"Unfortunately," Adams continued, "one isn't always wise enough. Or strong enough. And time passes and the moment is gone. Cinque, we're about to bring your case before the highest court in our land. We are about to do battle with a lion that is threatening to rip our country in two. And all we have on our side is a rock."

Cinque listened to the translation and when it

was over, he wondered if he would ever understand the way Americans talk.

"Of course, you didn't ask to be at the center of this historic conflagration any more than I did. But we find ourselves here nonetheless by some mysterious mix of circumstances with all the world looking on. What are we to do?"

Cinque finally interrupted and said to Covey, "Is he going to be any help at all? He seems to have far many more questions than answers."

"What did he say?" asked Adams.

Covey could not tell the former president what Cinque had really said. "Ah . . . I'm sorry, but I didn't catch it."

Adams decided not to press that and turned again to Cinque. "I'm being honest with you. Anything less would be disrespectful. I'm telling you, preparing you, I suppose, explaining to you that the task ahead of us is an exceptionally difficult one."

"We won't be going in there alone," Cinque said calmly.

"Indeed not. We have 'right' at our side. We have righteousness at our side. We have Baldwin over there."

Adams's droll wit was lost on Cinque. "I meant my ancestors."

Adams stared him.

"I will call into the past, far back to the beginning of time and beg them to come help me at the judgment. I will reach back and draw them into me. And they must come, for at this moment, I am the whole reason they have existed at all." Cinque met the white man's eyes. He couldn't tell for sure what Adams thought about what he'd said, but he had needed to say it. No one faced troubles alone. That was why there was family.

Adams regarded Cinque, now realizing that what he'd thought was really true. Cinque did represent a fierce manifestation of freedom. He was unwilling, unwilling indeed, to be brought into the system of slavery that had been intended for him. He obviously would fight against it on all fronts. He'd already killed for freedom. And now the American court system, from the lowest level to the highest, was concerned with his fate.

25

The Lion Comes
to Court

*"It is through asking questions that you
discover the truth."*

John Quincy Adams stood before the nine judges
of the Supreme Court, presided over by Chief Justice Roger Brooke Taney. Behind Adams sat Baldwin and Joadson, separated by Covey and
Cinque. Covey wasn't translating, which forced
Cinque to scour the room with his eyes. He
looked to each justice, to the lawyers, including
Holabird, the chief prosecutor. He watched the
faces of the spectators.

Outside the court, everyone had been bombarded by the unexpected level of intensity of the
protesting crowds, both for and against slavery. It
had finally hit Cinque how popular his fight to go
home had become. And that, after all was what it
was. He just wanted to go home. He had been
brought into this national argument about the enslavement of other human beings. All he knew
was that the slavery he'd experienced was noth-

ing like that which occurred back home. Slavery, like racism had been woven into the birth fabric of America. There were a lot of people who, either conscious or unconsciously, could not imagine this country surviving without either slavery or the racism that created it. And the fact that capitalism and the profit motive supported, even rewarded, the exploitation of people, it was easy to believe that everything would fall apart without it.

The former president spoke with a clear strong voice. It could shake the rafters if necessary or it could be as sweet as a seventy-two-year-old man's could be.

"Do we fear the lower courts, which found for us easily, somehow missed the truth? Is that it? Or is it rather our great and consuming fear of civil war that has allowed us to heap symbolism upon a simple case that never asked for it. And now would have us disregard truth even as it stands before us tall and proud as a mountain?

"The truth, in truth, has been driven from this case like a slave. Flogged from court to court, wretched and destitute. Not by any great legal acumen on the part of the opposition, but through the long, powerful arm of the Executive Office. Yea, this is no mere property case, gentleman. I put it to you thus: This is the most important case ever to come before this court. Because what it in fact concerns is the very nature of man."

Adams brought his hand behind his back and snapped his fingers. Baldwin delivered a sheaf of papers. "These are transcriptions of letters written between our secretary of state, John Forsyth, and the Queen of Spain, Isabella II. I ask that you include their perusal as part of your deliberations." He spread the papers out before Chief Justice Taney.

"I would not touch on them now except to note a curious phrase which is much repeated. The Queen, again and again, refers to our 'incompetent courts.' What, I wonder, would be more to her liking? A court that finds against the Africans? I think not. And here is the fine point of it: What Her Majesty wants is a court that behaves just like her court, the courts this nine-year-old child plays with in her magical kingdom called Spain. A court that will do what it is told. A court that can be toyed with like a doll. A court, as it happens, our own president could be proud of. If I could read you something . . ."

The court was still. Everyone watched the septaugenarian play his hand out in the court like a master, even though he had never been considererd an especially talented trial lawyer. Indeed, he was the first former president to appear before the Supreme Court in an official capacity. When John Quincy Adams became the courtroom lawyer, he commanded the attention of all who sat within the great hall of justice.

" 'The marshal of the United States will deliver over to Lieutenant John S. Paine of the United States Navy, and aid in conveying on board the vessel *Grampus*, under his command all the Negroes, late of the Spanish schooner *Amistad*, in his custody, under the process now pending before the District Court of the United States for the District of Connecticut. For so doing, this order will be his warrant. Given under my hand, at the city of Washington, this seventh day of January A.D. 1840. M. Van Buren.' "

He continued, now slowly stroking his whiskers. "Under process now pending, under process now pending," he said, as if in reflection. And then, to the court, "He had no intention of accepting a verdict of the district court contrary to his liking. He was going to put those people on that ship and convey them across seas to their deaths, no matter what the judge's ruling. Assuming a power no president has ever assumed before. A power no ruler, not in the most despotic governments of Europe would dare assume. And he didn't even try to hide it. I had no trouble at all procuring this. Which perhaps is as telling as this unprecedented document itself."

He approached the bench. He'd developed a three-pronged defense. The first simply to soften the justices up with Van Buren's arrogance. Get them wondering about his confidence in the judicial system.

"Will Your Honors please consider for one moment the essential principle of this order? Will you inquire, please, what, if it had been successfully carried out, would have been the tenure by which every citizen in this Union: man, woman, or child, would have held the blessing of personal freedom?"

He paused long enough to let his words sink in. "Now, I wish I could tell you the warship *Grampus* has been recalled to some other, less tyrannical duty. But it has not, Your Honors. It is standing by still, 'at the ready,' as this process is still pending. Because that is what our president thinks of your judgment."

And then it was time to take his argument to a different level. He walked back to the defense table and took a pamphlet that Baldwin offered. "I'd like to share something else with you. This is a publication of the Office of the President called the *Executive Review*. I'm sure you all read it. At least I'm sure the president hopes you all read it. This is a recent issue."

He began pacing, waving the publication in the air. Cinque watched him as did all the others. Some part of this, from the sheer dimensions of the room with its wood paneling and marble to the pageantry of the protocol seemed ridiculous. Even more so when he thought about the fact that one court had already set him free. But he was not free.

"And there is an article in here, written by a 'keen mind of the South,' my former vice president, John Calhoun, perhaps? Could it be? Who asserts that 'there has never existed a civilized society in which one segment did not thrive on the labor of another. As far back as one chooses to look, to ancient times, to biblical times, history bears this out. In Eden, where only two were created, even there, one was pronounced subordinate to the other. Slavery has always been with us and is neither sinful nor immoral. Rather, as war and antagonism are the natural states of man, so, too, slavery: as natural as it is inevitable.'

"Gentlemen, I must say I differ with the 'keen mind of the South,' and our president, who apparently shares their views, offering that the natural state of mankind is instead—and I know this is a controversial idea—freedom. And the proof is the lengths to which a man will go to regain it once taken." This was the second prong, an important point. He wanted to convince the court that a person was likely to do anything to reacquire their freedom when it was illegally taken.

"He will break loose his chains. He will decimate his enemies. He will try and try and try against all odds, against all adversity to get home."

He looked at Cinque and walked over to him.

"Stand up, Cinque, if you would, so everyone can see you." He gestured for Cinque to rise, which he did. After a long silence, Adams continued.

"This man is black. We can all see that. But can we also see as easily what is equally true? That he alone is the only true hero in this room? If he were white, he wouldn't be standing before this court fighting for his life. If he were white and his enslavers British, he wouldn't be able to stand, so heavy the weight of the medals we would bestow upon him. Songs would be written about him. The great authors of our time would fill books about him. His story would be told and retold in our classrooms. Our children, because we would make sure of it, would know his name as well as they know Patrick Henry's."

He then left Cinque standing there, receiving for the first time any real consideration as a man. It had taken a white man to give that to him. And he could feel it. He could feel the estimation of him grow in the room.

"Yet, if the South is right, what are we to do with this embarrassing document? This Constitution of the United States?" He said, pointing to a framed reproduction which hung on the wall. "In the minds of our congress, there seems to be little doubt. To keep me and any other from debating the legitimacy or morality of slavery, I've had the Constitution shoved in my mouth like a gag."

He moved then to a framed copy of the Declaration of Independence, which hung alongside the Constitution. "And what of this annoying document. What of its conceits? 'All men created equal . . . inalienable rights . . . life, liberty,' and so on and so forth? What on earth are we to do with this? I have a modest suggestion."

He'd thought about this moment the evening before and continued on with his plan. He tore up the *Executive Review* and let the pieces flutter to the floor. "I want to tell you a story. The other night I was talking with my friend, Cinque. He was over at my place. We were out in the greenhouse together. And he was explaining to me how, when a member of the Mende, his people, encounters a situation where there appears no hope at all, he invokes his ancestors.

"Tradition. The Mende believe that if one can summon the spirit of one's ancestors, then they have never left and that wisdom and strength they fathered will come to his aid." He then walked to a wall lined with portraits of famous Americans. "Thomas Jefferson. Benjamin Franklin. James Madison. Alexander Hamilton. George Washington. John Adams." He stopped there and stared at the picture of his father. Adams regarded the picture and seemed to be talking to it when he continued. "We have long resisted asking you for guidance. Perhaps we've feared in doing so, we might acknowledge that our individuality, which we so revere, is not entirely our own. Perhaps we've feared that an appeal to you might be taken for weakness. But we have to understand finally, that this is not so. We understand now." He looked at Cinque again. "We have been made to understand and to embrace the understanding that who we are is who we were.

"We desperately need your strength and wisdom to triumph over our fears, our prejudices, ourselves. Give us the courage to do what is right and if it means civil war? Then let it come. And when it does, may it be, finally, the last battle of the American Revolution." Finished, he slowly walked back to his chair and sat down. The courtroom was completely silent.

"That's all I have to say."

26
Verdict

"An empty bag cannot stand."

The night before the Supreme Court justices rendered their decision, was a night of restlessness and apprehension. It was a night of anticipation and hopefulness. But among all the principals of the *Amistad* case the most overlooked perhaps were the three girls who had become the wards of Mrs. Pendleton. Teme, Kahne, and Margru had endured the constant admonishments as they were molded into perfect little house servants. They had learned English well enough to sing hymns, to understand Mrs. Pendleton's Bible stories, and of course, to perform the many duties they were assigned around the house. And they had no idea what was happening in Washington, D.C.

They hadn't been told anything of the court proceedings or the struggle of Cinque to win their freedom. So as they shuttled from the kitchen to the sitting room with tea and cakes or turned down Mrs. Pendleton's bed or helped out in the kitchen, they could not know that nine judges were thinking of them.

Indeed, on this night it snowed in New Haven. The girls couldn't help being drawn to the window. Snow still held them spellbound. They stood there, smiling and pointing. The snow flakes were as large as popcorn and nearly as fluffy as it drifted down around them.

Behind them Mrs. Pendleton entertained one of her many aristocratic friends, who often visited just to see the progress she'd made with the little African girls. And it was at these moments that Mrs. Pendleton was the most conscious of her importance: to the community and to the girls. She was the only one thing that separated them from the uncivilized life they'd left behind. And look what she'd been able to do. *Look at them,* she thought. All anybody had to do was look at them to see how much work she'd put into them.

When they turned away from the window, still full of wonder of New England in winter, they came face-to-face with Mrs. Pendleton, who'd caught them dawdling there. When they saw her, each of them froze and lowered their heads and left the room. Mrs. Pendleton had insisted that when she entertained, they were to avoid eye contact with her or her guests.

This was one of the problems. The Pendletons

were not unusual in that whatever compassion they had toward black people somehow always seemed to render them into subservience.

Across the courtyard Buakei paced in his cell. He knew things were happening. He knew that Cinque had gone to get their freedom back. He stopped and slipped each arm between the bars and let the snow softly pelt the palms of his hands. He brought a little to his mouth and tasted the coldness. Up and down the cell block other hands reached out. And voices sang. And among some of them, there was much talk about going home. Among others, there was a certainty that they were headed back to Cuba aboard the ship that sat out in the harbor.

It was snowing in Washington as well that night. Cinque watched the flakes move past the window of his jail cell. He'd been standing there for a long time staring into the Washington night sky. How far he'd come in his desire to return home. How long could a man survive away from his home? When does the moment come when he no longer seeks to find "home" and accepts the fact that he is already there? Wasn't that what had happened to Joadson? To Covey? And all of the other black Americans he'd seen, most of them servants. Did they feel at home when the day was done?

It wasn't for him. He'd never forget where his ancestors were. Where his family was. That would always be his home. He wouldn't rest until he was back there.

Not far away, Baldwin also stood staring out of a window. He'd been in his hotel most of the evening. He watched the snow settle over Washington. This case had been nothing like he'd expected it would be. At first it was a simple property dispute, easily tried, easily won. The Africans were not the property of the Spanish and indeed, had not been born into slavery. That meant they were free. He'd had no idea of the intense feelings aroused by the existence of slavery or any serious discussion about ending it.

And that's what the *Amistad* case had become. A discussion about the validity and the morality of human bondage. And when it reached that level of intensity, it had passed beyond his competence to argue. He'd really needed John Quincy Adams or someone like him to make this argument. America was in no mood to quibble about slavery. Only a venerated, some might even say doddering, ex-president could have stood up to the pressures that were obvious and evident.

From the moment he'd been punched in the hallway of the New Haven court house, until this day as they waited for the Supreme Court to finish their deliberations, he'd realized his own limitations. And he had them. He was passionate, yes, but he was also privileged. He went home a free white man every day. Cinque had always been under lock and key. And what about Joadson? Joadson was a free black American and yet, he had always had to defer to that privilege. He always had to guard what he said, how he said it, and to whom he was speaking. That was a fact of life, even for a free black American.

But in the process, Baldwin had to admit that he'd learned a lot. He'd learned that he didn't want to be like some abolitionists who put their fight for salvation ahead of the true needs of the wretched. Yet the abolitionists were so important. They'd made the fight possible. Without a growing number of white Americans who were disgusted enough with the institution of slavery and what it was doing to their country, who could guess how long it would last? So he was happy to have been a part of this case. But he was glad that they'd finally gotten Adams involved. Baldwin thought about turning in. He wasn't certain he could actually sleep. His stomach was suddenly unsteady.

And not more than three blocks away Adams sat up in his bed. He was more than fatigued. Exhausted. His throat was hoarse, his joints ached from all the strutting and gesturing. At the moment, he didn't care that much one way or the other. He just wanted to rest. Still he couldn't get Cinque's face out of his mind. The regal African sitting before the Supreme Court. He wanted justice for Cinque. It had obviously been a tragedy from the start. The kidnapping, being sold into slavery, the mutiny, the capture. The trial. All Cinque had done was walk off his farm one day.

He blew out the flame of his candle and lay flat. Slavery was wrong. There was no other way to look at it. Cinque had a family. He had a life that should have been his own to determine. The promise of America could not become a reality until the issue of race was settled. The beginning of that could only begin with the end of slavery.

The next morning everyone was in place as the justices entered the courtroom. The room was packed with spectators. The chill that had enveloped Washington was lost in this room. With the people and the level of emotions, it was actually quite warm.

And then Justice Story, who wrote the opinion, began. "In the case of the United States of America *versus* the *Amistad* Africans, it is an opinion of this court that our treaty of 1795 with Spain, on which the prosecution has primarily based its arguments, is applicable.

"While it is clearly stipulated in Article 9 that 'seized ships and cargo are to be returned entirely to their proprietary,' it has not been shown to the court's satisfaction that these particular Africans fit that description. We are left then with the alternative: That they are not slaves, and therefore cannot be considered merchandise . . ."

Covey had been translating for Cinque, who understood the moment and tried on a cautious smile. Baldwin could feel it rising in him, as could everyone at the defense table. Adams suddenly seemed unconcerned.

". . . but are rather free individuals with certain legal and moral rights, including the right to engage in insurrection against those who would deny them their freedom. Therefore, it is our judgment, with one dissension that the defendants are to be released from custody at once. And, if they so choose, be returned to their homes in Africa."

Justice Story brought the gavel down and the courtroom dispersed. There was a rising level of confusion as the spectators began making their exit. Adams did not outwardly show what he felt. In many ways he was as proud of this moment as any in his career. He looked at Baldwin, a mixture of humility and arrogance, and flashed the slightest of smiles.

Cinque looked up as a federal marshal began unlocking his manacles and chains. He felt them fall away. And then Adams was beside him and Cinque asked him in Mende, "What did you say to them? What words did you use to persuade them?"

Covey translated and Adams nodded. He then said directly to Cinque, "Yours." And, as he heard Covey's translation, Adams extended his hand. Cinque took it and gave it a vigorous shake, obviously mimicking the way Americans did.

Joadson walked up and offered his hand to Cinque, who fumbled with something a second before switching his attention from Adams. When Cinque closed his hand over his, Joadson could feel Cinque place something in his palm. It was the charm that he'd managed to keep through it all. And, when it was lost, Joadson had found it and returned it to him. Now he wanted Joadson to have it. He might need it more than Cinque did now.

"To keep you safe."

Joadson didn't know what to say. He fingered the charm and immediately felt the depth of history and tradition which seemed woven into it. He didn't know that it was Cinque's wife's present to him. He didn't know that it represented something so basic, so elemental and fundamental as family and home. That was what she had given to Cinque and now he was giving it to Joadson. In a way, the differences between them weren't that great. Perhaps they were like two men of different tribes who happened to meet under stressful circumstances. One of them had decided to help the other one find his way home. Two tribes. Two languages. Perhaps even two cultures recognizing what was common between them. Why they really were brothers.

And then Cinque's eyes met Baldwin's, who was separated from the African by a fair number of people. But he stood there patiently, waiting for the moment when they would congratulate each other. Inside, Baldwin was as excited as he'd ever been in his life. He smiled as Cinque broke from the crowd and began making his way toward him.

Cinque was overwhelmed suddenly by the sense of freedom that he felt. There were no chains, no guards, no bars, no cells. As the minutes passed, he became more and more giddy.

As Baldwin and Cinque shook hands, Cinque said in English, "Thank you."

Baldwin pulled Cinque's hand to his chest, in Mende fashion and, in Mende, said back to him, "Thank you, Sengbe." Baldwin held him there as people gathered around them. This was the delivery of the big promise. One man's commitment to the other in a struggle of self-definition and freedom.

During the Supreme Court hearing, President Van Buren received regular reports from Forsyth. When Adams had made his great performance before the court, he knew they were in trouble.

Verdict

The Southern states would never support him now. Calhoun hadn't been bluffing and he knew it. This case, among the many other struggles of his administration, had become another nail in the coffin of the troubled Van Buren presidency.

Slavery would be the blade that cut through the muscle of America. There was a part of him that cheered the Court and their brave decision. There was a measure of respect for his adversary, John Quincy Adams. But more than anything else, he wanted to eradicate the evidence of the whole miserable enterprise the *Amistad* case had become.

So when Forsyth suggested they ask the Queen of England for use of her African squadron to find and destroy the slave factories, beginning with Galinas Bay, that dotted the coast of West Africa, he agreed. Blast the slaveholders. Blast them all.

27

To Home Free

" 'Had I only known' is always an afterthought."

"In the name of the Father and the Son and the Holy Ghost. I christen thee," was what Yamba heard as his conversion was made complete in waist-deep water, in a New England river. He'd traveled his own full circle. His movement to Christ, though nearly unfathomable two years before seemed almost natural now. Yamba had needed a force stronger than the ancestors, stronger than Cinque, stronger than any charm or amulet. He had needed the word of God. And now he was immersed and anointed. Within the arms of his new God, there was a peacefulness he'd never known. A sense of joy and anticipation of the future that was without limit or qualification. He was truly free.

He was going home.

As were the rest of his people, although they were once again aboard a ship, a merchant ship, the *Gentleman*. They were gathered on deck, including the three girls who had exchanged their American dresses for pantaloons and shirts. Covey was also aboard, minus his British uniform. He'd decided to retire from the Royal Navy and go back home with the others.

Cinque walked to the bow of the ship and stood there, staring ahead. There, at the edge of the horizon was the sun, beckoning to him. That was the way home. He could now hear his wife calling to him. The same chant he'd heard the day he was captured. He'd heard it again in the moments before he'd decided to take matters into his own hands on the *Amistad*. He'd never stopped hearing it. And now, finally he was sailing home. There and back again.

Cinque left behind an America that was on the verge of being ripped apart by war, a war that was fought largely around the issue of slavery. He left behind a country that had made itself great with the forced help of African sweat. A country which used these men and women like animals, destroyed their families, took their identities from them, and broke them. Literally broke their will to be independent human beings, transforming them into slaves. And yet, from what Cinque had seen, the fire and strength of Africa still beat within their chests. He felt that the Tappans and the Joadsons would not stop until the chains of slavery no longer clanked in America.

He couldn't help wondering whether there were men like him among them. Men who would take the chance and risk death for freedom. These American Africans would need men and women who were willing to die for it.

But he also knew that "home" was a delicate idea. Nearly as fragile as life itself. You could take someone from their home and deprive them of everything that recalled "home" and after a while, where you were became your home. He'd seen it. He'd been there, and were it not for a group of committed people and the forces of nature and God, he would not be going back to the place he truly knew was home. Africa.

> We journey across the waters,
> Away from the great cold,
> Back home, back home.
>
> I pray to see my mother,
> I pray to see my father,
> I pray to see my children,
> Back home, back home.

Epilogue

There was a way in which the reality that had become Cinque's world had been like a painting. It was as if someone had been furiously painting a massive canvas which draped the background of his life in images he'd never on his own be able to imagine. The colors had been muted. Mostly dark and forbidding browns and sinister greens with stripes of red peeking through.

Now that the nightmare was over, Cinque often dreamed about *being* at home. When he was a captive, all of his conscious and unconscious energy was focused on *going* back home. But more and more he'd found himself here, in Mani, at peace. There was however an unsettling detail in all of his dreams. No matter where he was, in the field, in his house, in the village, there was always a shadow lurking just beyond his scope of vision. Each time he awoke, he'd find his hands tightly clenched and sweat riding his forehead.

He knew what it was. It would always be there. In his head. In the stories about him. The lion, a symbol of strength and power felled by a rock thrown from his own hand. It was a dream that would be forever his. And as uneasy dreams go, this one wasn't so terrible. At least he had destroyed the lion.

Little did Cinque know that he had helped to also destroy the tools of his abduction. For, at roughly the same time that Cinque prepared to make his voyage across the expansive Atlantic, back at the slave factory in Lomboko, on the Galinas Bay, the great *barracoon* of Don Blanco was suddenly under a ground attack by the British Marines.

The *barracoon* guards who stood atop the towers that overlooked the bay and the hillside which rolled down toward the Atlantic were taken completely by surprise. They could do little more than fire at the waves of British soldiers as they stormed the gates.

Most of the guards fell quickly from the return fire of the British muskets. Those that didn't, could only watch as the gates were ripped open and the lines of soldiers took position and fired into the *barracoon*. Slavers and guards dropped in the perpetually muddy yard of the factory. This was the same ground that Cinque had sat on, tired and hungry before the trip to Cuba. And now it was being torn apart. The only better justice would have been for the Africans from the *Amistad* and all the others who had begun their journey there to have been present as the soldiers broke open the slave cells and released the captives who issued into the fresh air like steam. They had no idea that their freedom could be traced directly to the *Amistad* case.

Off the coast sat a British cruiser commanded by Captain Fitzgerald, the same man who had lent Ensign Covey to the *Amistad* legal team and who had played some role in the way the case turned out. Now he stood on the bridge of the ship awaiting a signal from shore. His quartermaster stood next to him with his telescope focused on the gates of the slave factory. Finally, there was a flash of light that emanated from the beach.

"Clear, sir," the quartermaster said.

Captain Fitzgerald stiffened his back and calmly said. "Fire." And the word "fire" bounced about deck like a ball. Within a minute the ship's cannons thundered in a sequence from forward to aft along the starboard. The captain then took the telescope from the quartermaster and watched the cannon shot drop down on the slave factory. The cells that had begun the journey of death and bondage were destroyed, one by one.

The cannons were now silent. Now the captain broke a smile. "Load and fire." The ship's crew responded with a flurry of activity until the cannons roared once more. Ashore, the structures that Don Blanco had built and fortified were blasted to pieces. Iron flew and the shards from the timbers that had been driven into the ground danced around like birds in flight. And this was repeated until there was nothing left of the Galinas *barracoon* but rubble.

"Take a letter, Ensign," Captain Fitzgerald called to his clerk as he walked into his cabin.

"Yes, sir."

"To His Honor, United States Secretary of State, John Forsyth. My dear Mr. Forsyth, it is my great pleasure to inform you that you are, in fact, correct. The slave factory in Sierra Leone does not exist." The captain looked to shore. Above the area where the *barracoon* had once stood was a massive cloud of smoke. It rolled up into itself.

Captain Fitzgerald watched as the cloud seemed to form a familiar shape. He smiled. There was the head, the mane, the muscular body, and then a trail of smoke that could easily have been the tail. And with the continuing explosions erupting below it, it could well have been the last roar.

He'd been more than happy to do this for the American president.